SO YOU LOVE YOUR BEST FRIEND'S SISTER

SO YOU WANT TO BE A BILLIONAIRE BOOK 3

ELIZABETH MADDREY

1

Jessica Ward spotted her brother, Christopher, across the conference room as she slipped through the door. She wasn't late, at least. She'd gotten caught up in a problem for one of her customers and had silenced the phone alarm she'd set for the meeting. Then kept on coding.

She crossed the room and pulled out the seat beside Christopher.

Her brother glanced at her, and his eyebrows lifted. "Jess? You're here?"

Of course, he was surprised. He was constantly underestimating her. Which was fine—she didn't actually mind. Sure, it might be nice for him to take her seriously as an adult, but as big brothers went, he was a keeper. She spotted Ryan across the room and ignored the tiny frisson of awareness that always hit her right in the gut when it came to her brother's best friend. "Best of the best, you know it. Ry's getting coffee."

Ryan took the seat beside her and leaned around to nod at Christopher.

"Hey, Ryan."

Christopher introduced the woman next to him. So this was

Stephanie. Not at all what she'd imagined from her brother's griping about working with her. She was pretty. Serious, though. And ugh, why did he insist on always labeling Jess as his little sister?

"Hi. Jessica Ward. I'd prefer not to be known as Christopher's sister whenever possible." Jessica held out her hand with a friendly grin. There was no point in judging the woman by her brother's standard when Jess didn't have the background to know if it was accurate or not.

At least Stephanie laughed. Then turned her attention to Ryan—which was all the excuse Jess needed to shift and look at him, too. Why did he have to be so dreamy? He'd taken to wearing a neatly trimmed five o'clock shadow lately. It added that hint of sleepy just-rolled-out-of-bed to his look, and she wasn't sure if she wanted to tuck him back in or just hug him really tight.

Of course, he was off-limits.

Was that why she was interested?

No one was safer than the guy who was off-limits.

Ryan and Chris had been best pals since they met in the fourth grade, and they'd pegged Jess firmly into the annoying little sister role since day one. Nothing gave either of them more joy than chasing her around with a frog or trying to put an earthworm on her arm.

She fought a shudder.

"You okay?" Ryan leaned close, his breath tickling her ear.

Darn shivers. She nodded, not trusting her voice.

"If you'd all find a seat, we can get started." Joe Robinson, the company owner and CEO, grinned as he took the chair at the head of the conference table and settled in it. The few stragglers who'd been by the coffee all made their way to the table. "Good. Great. Thanks, everyone, for making time in your day to attend this meeting."

Jess rolled her eyes. Like anyone was going to say no. This contest—and who would be invited to participate—had been the talk of the water cooler since Joe announced his plan to step back from directly managing all five arms of Robinson Enterprises and, instead, to choose employees to take over for him by way of a contest. There were teams of two—but it seemed that only one team member would win. The other? Maybe a subordinate role? Jess supposed they'd find out as part of this meeting.

She hadn't expected to get an invitation. Honestly, she'd been surprised anyone outside of the cyber security division knew who she was. Inside? Sure, she had a reputation as someone who could solve problems, but it wasn't as if she was running around gaining notoriety.

Joe kept talking. Sounded like Tyler Shaw—Joe's right-hand man—was going to be more in charge than Joe himself. That was fine. She liked Tyler.

Joe paused, then continued. "One of the biggest measurements of success is going to be how the two of you work together to achieve it."

Jess glanced over at Ryan and grinned. That sounded perfect —much better than a ton of individual tasks with them pitted against each other. They made a good team. It'd be like when they were kids—except this time they'd be on the same side. At least until the end, when, hopefully, she'd come out on top. She glanced down at the faded jeans and graphic tee layered over a thermal shirt that she'd pulled on this morning. Maybe she should have planned ahead a little more and dressed up.

Ryan had.

He was wearing khakis and a blue Oxford, which he hardly ever did. Jess had seen him in a suit a time or two, but that was when he had a big client meeting. He looked good no matter what he wore. But she was definitely not going to object if he started dressing up more.

Dang it, she'd missed the rest of Joe's speech. Something about synergy and monthly meetings. Had he said their first task? Ry wasn't going let her hear the end of it if she'd missed that.

"You don't have a competitor."

Jess winced at Stephanie's tone. Gutsy statement, but honestly, why would she put a target on her back like that?

Tyler sent Stephanie a long, cool look. "No. I don't. It's mine unless I screw up. There are reasons behind that decision, but I'm reasonably sure if Joe felt you needed to know what they were, he'd tell you."

If she could, Jess would find a way to help Stephanie disappear—it sure looked like that was what the other woman wished would happen. Jess didn't blame her one bit. Even if she'd brought it on herself with her statement.

Then the meeting was over. Tyler had packets for them to pick up on their way out.

Jess looked for her brother, but he was already sliding through the crowd. She shrugged and tilted her head toward the folders. "I'll grab ours. Wanna meet in my cube?"

Ryan shook his head. "Why don't you get your computer and come to my office? I have a door and an actual table."

"Yeah, yeah." Jess grinned. She'd figured he'd say that, but she didn't mind her cube.

"You have anything pressing today? Or do you think we can take an hour or two now and kick around some ideas?"

There was always work. She shrugged. "I can make the time. Give me twenty?"

"Yeah." Ryan tapped his forehead and started toward the door.

Jess waited as the other teams took their folders. Finally, she made her way up and laid claim to the last one. "Thanks, Tyler."

"Sure. Good luck."

She frowned as she eyed him. "You okay? How's Danielle?"

Tyler's smile flashed, but it didn't hit his eyes. "She's back at work."

"That's good, right?"

"I guess. There's still a lot of memory loss for recent events—but she's been in her role long enough she's been able to pick that back up with relative ease."

Jess frowned. Danielle had been in a bad car accident, but Jess hadn't heard anything about brain injury. "Sorry. I'll keep praying. For both of you."

"Appreciate it. Definitely let me know if you have questions. You're paired with Ryan?"

"Yep. Should be a cakewalk."

Tyler chuckled. "I like a positive attitude. See ya."

Jess clutched the folder and followed him from the now-empty conference room. She'd make a pit stop, grab her laptop, and then hit Ryan's office.

Maybe working together on this project would, finally, let Ryan see her as a woman and not just his best friend's annoying sister.

If it didn't?

Jess shook her head. She didn't even want to go there.

RYAN FOSTER FROWNED out his office window. Traffic was already picking up—maybe a lot of people were taking a late lunch? It seemed early for anyone to be leaving for the day. Of course, there was always traffic in Tyson's Corner, so maybe that was all it was.

He scrubbed a hand over his face.

This was going to be awful.

Jess Ward.

What were Joe and Tyler thinking?

Oh, sure, she was capable. Honestly, she was probably one of the best employees in Cyber. But Christopher Ward was practically a brother to Ryan, which made Jess the same thing as a sister.

And he should *not* feel this way about his kid sister.

He turned from the window, squeezing his hands into fists and stretching them out. He could do this. He *would* do this. He had to, if for no other reason than Jess couldn't win. There was no way they'd be able to continue getting contracts from government agencies and the contractors who supported the government if the whole division was run by one of the top five hackers in the United States. As it was, there were sometimes problems.

Oh sure, she'd never been caught, but he knew for certain that the FBI had their suspicions, because they dragged him out to lunch every eight to ten weeks to see if they could weasel information out of him.

Jess hadn't done anything bad—no stealing, no destruction, nothing like that—but she'd been too good at uncovering security vulnerabilities and hadn't been shy about pointing them out. Publicly. A fact that other hackers with more questionable morals had happily taken advantage of.

Chris had worked hard to get her to sign on here as a last-ditch effort to get her to go straight. Then he'd tasked Ryan with keeping an eye on his little sister. And the feelings Ryan had developed while doing so were going to have to go with him to his grave. Keep her out of trouble? Yes. Fall in love with her? Definitely not what Chris had in mind.

"Hey." Jess poked her head in the door with a grin. Her eyes were bright and full of laughter. "You ready?"

"Yeah, come on in." Ryan worked to arrange his features into an easy smile—he'd gotten good at putting on his game face. He rubbed his hands together and slipped around his desk to the small round table that filled the bulk of his office. "What've we got?"

Jess set down her laptop, dropped a folder on top of it, then sat. "I don't know. I figured we should look together. They made a big deal about collaboration in the meeting this morning. I didn't want to cheat."

Ryan laughed. "I'm pretty sure looking over what they gave us wouldn't have violated any of the rules, but whatever. You want a soda?"

"Sure. I forget you keep a stash. I don't imagine you have anything diet?"

He snorted as he went back around his desk to the mini fridge he kept tucked under one corner. "Please, you don't need diet soda. And I'm pretty sure I read that artificial sweeteners are bad for you."

"Sure. So is sugar. And caffeine. And really just about anything that's delicious." Jess shrugged and took the can from him when he offered it. She popped the top and took a swig. "Mmm. Gotta say, this tastes better than diet."

"Right?" He opened his own soda and sipped as he sat. "All right, flip open that folder."

Jess shook her head as she did. She angled it between them on the table. "So, a list of meeting dates and the teams, some rah-rah documentation about the company, and the fine print about the competition. Nothing exciting."

Ryan stopped her before she could slap it closed. "Don't you think we ought to read the fine print? I'm a big fan of knowing what I'm getting into."

"I guess. You'd really back out if you saw something in there you didn't like?"

Would he? "I mean, yeah. I don't think Joe would ask any of us to do something illegal or unethical, but I want to be sure, first. Trust but verify, you know?"

She rolled her eyes and took another sip of soda.

He shrugged and scanned the document. There wasn't anything super surprising—except . . . he tapped the bottom of the page. "See here?"

Jess craned her neck and frowned as she read. "So we can go through everything over the next six months, and he still might not choose one of us to head things up? That's unfair."

"It's his company." Ryan didn't like it, but at the end of the day, Joe could do what he wanted. "Anyway, knowing that should shape how we do this. We need to make sure we follow everything they say to improve our chances of winning and actually being awarded the prize."

"Yeah, okay. I was going to do that, anyway."

"Me, too. But still." He took a quick sip of soda and flipped the folder closed. "I'd half considered divvying up the business plan, but given this?" He tapped the folder. "Let's just do it all together."

"Sure. Should we start now?" Jess reached for her laptop.

"I can swing an hour. Maybe first, let's look at our schedules and see when we can set time aside to get together consistently." Ryan pulled his phone out of his pocket and navigated to the calendar. Man, he had a lot of meetings. Sure, it was part of having the position he did, but he missed the thrill of chasing security leaks or solving the hard problems that came with contracts. Stephanie had said some of the work he'd helped write up had been shifted over to Cyber, and he really would love to have a chance to help. The customer had a unique setup that was going to be tricky to navigate. He sighed. None of that made finding time to spend with Jess easier. "Wednesdays are my best days."

"I can do Wednesdays if it's late afternoon."

Ryan scowled at his calendar. "We might have to get together after hours."

"Okay."

He looked up at her. "Just like that?"

"Sure. This is important. I'll make the time. Why? You don't want to give up your busy dating schedule?" Jess smirked at him.

Ryan's face heated. People around the office had the impression he kept a string of girls on the hook, never getting serious or committing to any of them. He wasn't completely sure how it happened, but he hadn't done anything to set the record straight, either. Being seen as unavailable had stopped the pointed flirting from some of the women in the office. And it had given him one more tool in his quest to keep Jess at arm's length. "I'm sure it'll be fine."

Her eyebrows lifted. "Are you? That's not what I've heard."

"C'mon, Jess. You know me." Ryan shook his head. She could think what she wanted. "Whatever. Anyway, Wednesday after work? Should we start with that?"

She frowned a little, looking like she was going to say something else, then shook her head. "Yeah, okay. And we have an hour now. Right?"

"We do. There are probably little pockets of time throughout the week—maybe just email in the morning to let me know when you have a little time, and I'll see what gels for me?" It might make more sense for him to check in with her every morning, but she got to work earlier than he did most days. If she reached out first thing, then he could find time more easily as soon as he arrived.

"I can do that." Jess flipped open her laptop and dragged her finger back and forth across the touchpad until the screen lit. "So. A business plan. This may shock you, but I've never written a business plan."

Ryan chuckled. "That does not, in fact, shock me. I haven't either. But Tyler was going to send out a template, so that should help. If it's not here yet, we could poke around online and see what we find that way."

"I don't have the email yet. Did you get it?"

Ryan opened the email app on his phone and dragged down to refresh. "Just came. Check yours again."

"There it is. Okay." She clicked a few times before scooting closer to Ryan and shifting her laptop. She wrinkled her nose.

Ryan tried not to stare at the light dusting of freckles visible now that she was closer. He tried not to breathe in her fresh scent. She didn't wear perfume—it was just soap and water. But it made him crazy. Crazy enough that he'd actually asked Christopher, who had in turn asked Jess, all under the guise of wanting to get some for his mom for Christmas.

That backfired badly.

Her elbow jabbed his arm. "Where'd you go?"

"Huh?"

Jess laughed. "Seriously, man, I asked like three questions about this business plan but you were off in la-la land. You okay?"

"Yeah. I'm good. "He was also an idiot who needed to focus. "What'd you ask?"

"Where do we start? At the top and work down? Do we pick and choose? I don't even know how to tackle something like this, there was no 'how to write a business plan' course in my programming undergrad."

Her *unfinished* undergrad. He wasn't going to add that, but it always seemed like a waste to him. She should have the degree. And probably a Master's, as well. Ryan took a breath. "Scroll down to the table of contents, and let me think."

Jess scrolled.

He leaned closer so he could see.

His heart thundered in his chest, and his mouth went dry.

This wasn't going to work. There was no way this could

work. Even if Jess was interested in him, which she very clearly wasn't, Christopher would kill both of them. Probably more than once.

Focus, man.

Ryan shrugged. "Let's start at the top and work down. If that's wrong, we'll probably figure it out on the way."

Jess snickered. "You hope."

Yeah. Maybe while he was figuring out the business plan, he could also figure out once and for all how to stop being attracted to his best friend's sister.

Because acting on that was out of the question.

2

Ryan hit Send on the email and scooted away from his desk. Jess would be coming in another ten minutes to work on their business plan. He'd spent a little time researching the language expected for documents like this. He didn't have an MBA. He didn't have a cyber security degree, either, but at least he knew IT. The business world? Everything he knew about management came from books and podcasts.

It was working for him so far, but he really wanted to win this contest.

Having Jess as his second in command wouldn't be terrible either.

Unless it was.

Christopher and he ran a men's Bible study at their condo on Mondays. This week, Ryan had barely managed to stay focused enough to joke around during the inevitable chicken dinner that Christopher had brought home with him. The study had been good—all of the guys were part of the contest in their various departments, so the question of what it profited a man to gain the world if he lost his soul? It had left them all quiet.

The salary package that came with the promotion—and the

responsibility—was a big lure. Was it wrong to want those things? He had good motives. Didn't he?

"Hey, ready?" Jess stood in the doorway, grinning. "Or were you going to sit there zoning out for another five minutes?"

"I wasn't zoning. I was thinking."

"Uh-huh." She strode into the room and started to situate herself at the table.

She had her usual uniform of jeans, a long-sleeved thermal, and a graphic T-shirt over the top. Today's shirt was red, featuring a picture of a black box with the caption "The Internet."

"You're not staring at my chest, right? Cause I'm going to go out on a limb and say that's not super cool." Jess waggled her eyebrows.

Heat flooded his face, and he looked away. "I was trying to understand your shirt."

"Seriously? Do you not actually watch the TV shows I recommend to you?" Jess shook her head and popped open her laptop. "You're missing out."

"Some of us don't have a lot of time for lazing around."

"Please. Lazing around. It's background noise while I . . ." Jess trailed off and cleared her throat. "Anyway, I did some poking around online. Have you read a business plan? They're kind of snooty."

What had she been going to say? The sinking sensation in his stomach went along with the thought that it was probably something to do with hacking. She was always very careful to avoid saying she'd quit. When pressed, she could give a forceful argument for why white-hat hacking was a good thing. Except, as far as their clients were concerned, there was no difference. Should he say something? Not yet. "I think what you mean is 'formal.'"

"No. I mean snooty. They talk around things rather than

being concise and clear." Jess dug a piece of gum out of her pocket, unwrapped it, and popped it in her mouth. "So you might need to be the one typing. I can give you ideas, and you can massage the language."

"Massage the language?" Ryan laughed. "What makes you think I'm going to be better at that than you are?"

"You have two degrees. You have to be better at it than a college dropout." She pushed the laptop toward him.

"I guess we'll see." Ryan pulled the computer to himself and flexed his fingers. "Okay, let's get started."

They worked steadily for two hours. Once they got going, it was easy—well fine, easy*ish*—for Ryan to concentrate on the document and not the warmth radiating off Jess, or the clean, sunshiny scent she brought with her everywhere she went.

He paused and leaned back in his chair. "What do you think?"

"I think it's a start, and my brain hurts." She twisted the smart watch on her wrist. "Also that it's time for dinner. You want to grab something?"

Ryan fought to keep his expression bland. "I could eat."

"You don't have something with Chris tonight? I know the two of you do roommate stuff. I don't want to horn in."

He laughed. "No. No roommate stuff planned. Let's wrap up and grab eats."

"What are you in the mood for?"

Now there was a dangerous question. She had no idea. He cleared his throat. "I don't know, burger?"

"Yeah, okay. I want boardwalk fries though." Jess shut down the laptop and closed the lid. "I need to grab some stuff from my cube. Five Guys?"

"Sure. Meet you there in twenty?"

Jess considered a moment before nodding. "I guess that's what it'll take with parking and everything."

"Yep. Unless you want to share a ride? It'd mean carpooling tomorrow, too." He held his breath. Jess could get prickly about the fact that she lived in the same building they did. Ryan always hated that their schedules made it tricky to commute together. And they weren't near the Metro, so public transit was out.

"We can do that. You're sure you don't mind?"

He shook his head.

"Okay. I still need to grab stuff from my cube. I'll meet you at the elevators in five?"

"That works." Ryan stood.

Jess waved as she tucked her laptop under her arm and headed out of his office.

Ryan pumped his fist. Dinner was a good start. Not that this was a date. It was just smart planning and a chance to grab some food.

Maybe if he kept reminding himself of that, he wouldn't get his hopes up.

Oh, who was he kidding?

If his hopes got any higher, they'd be in orbit.

He shook his head and collected up what he needed to take home, then headed toward the elevators. There was no sense in keeping her waiting.

JESS IGNORED her quivering belly as she hurried through the mostly-deserted rows of cubes back to hers. She'd managed to snag a spot near the windows, so at least she had some natural light—but it was far from the elevators.

Most of the time she didn't mind.

But she didn't want to keep Ryan waiting. Not when they were finally getting a chance to share a meal without her brother around.

Oh, sure, she'd eaten with Ryan a ton of times, but always as one of the guys. And okay, that was a big step up from the annoying little sister, but still. Maybe that was what this was, too, but at least there was no crowd this time.

Delusional.

Jess shook her head. Ryan didn't think of her like that. Why did she hold onto the idea that someday he might?

She sighed and packed up her bag.

At least she'd get a good burger and some peanut-oil fries out of it. She wasn't going to think about the workout the meal would require, either. The building their condos were in had a good fitness center in the basement. Hardly anyone ever used it, too, which made it even nicer. Adding an extra mile onto her usual wasn't a hardship. And maybe she'd be tired enough that she wouldn't be able to continue obsessing over Ryan.

She really needed to get a life.

Possibly a date.

Jess hurried to the elevators.

Ryan was already there, and his grin lit up his whole face when he spotted her. "I was wondering if I was going to have to send out a search party."

"Har, har." Jess rolled her eyes and concentrated on sticking to playful banter, despite the lazy roll her heart gave. She was used to that by now. His smile had been wreaking havoc on her system for the last seven years. Minimum. The worst part? It was like he had no idea. She was just his best friend's kid sister. The one who always wanted to tag along, even when she was clearly not wanted.

"Should we see what Chris is doing? He's always up for a burger." Ryan glanced over at her.

Jess swallowed her disappointment and ignored the bitter taste it left in her mouth. "Yeah, sure. Why not? He can fill us in on how things are going with his partner."

Ryan snickered.

The elevator chimed as it arrived at their floor. Jess punched the parking garage button with a little too much force. Should she change her mind and just meet him at the burger place? Parking was such a nightmare, though. Carpooling really did make more sense. Ugh.

When the door slid open again, Ryan pointed. "I'm over that way."

"Missed out on your usual spot this morning, I see?"

His eyebrows shot up.

"What?"

"I didn't realize I had a regular spot."

Her cheeks burned. She jerked one shoulder. "I feel like I'm always trying to squeeze past your behemoth on my way to the elevator."

"Behemoth?" Ryan patted the front corner of his SUV. "She's not that big. Seats four and only really if the people in the back seat aren't picky about legroom. You should know that—you've whined about being squeezed back there often enough."

"Yeah, well. *It* still doesn't fit in the compact-cars-only spaces that are near the elevators." She smirked at him and reached for the passenger door handle. So far, he hadn't tried to call her brother to invite him. Maybe he'd forget.

"She." Ryan frowned, his head shaking. "You're going to hurt her feelings if you're not careful."

"Uh-huh. Does she have a name, too?" What was it with men and their cars? Jess clicked her seatbelt into place and stretched out her legs. It really was much nicer in the front. No wonder Chris was always calling shotgun—even though that was a completely juvenile move at this stage of life—when they went somewhere with Ryan.

"Duh." Ryan started the car and eased out of the parking spot.

Jess waited a moment before speaking again. "And that name is?"

"None of your business."

She studied his face. Were his cheeks pink? Well, well. He was embarrassed. That could be fun. "Hmm. A mystery. That makes me want to dig. You know that, right?"

"You're such a pest." He swiped his access card and drove under the security arm as soon as it lifted enough for him to get through. When they reached the stop sign at the end of the garage ramp, he tapped his phone. Moments later, ringing filled the car.

"This is Christopher."

"Hey, man, it's Ry. Jess and I are going to hit up burgers and fries. You want in?" Ryan punched the gas, and the SUV shot smoothly out into traffic.

Jess fought a sigh. So much for that. Now she just had to pray her brother had better things to do. Maybe he and Stephanie would be working on their five-year plan and wouldn't want prying eyes and ears. She and Ryan wouldn't copy them, but they didn't know that.

"Nah, but thanks. I'm enjoying the quiet. Have fun. Oh, hey, before you go."

"Yeah?" Ryan flicked on his turn signal.

"How are things going with Jess? This whole business with the contest isn't too much for her?"

Ryan winced and glanced over at Jess.

She shook her head and held a finger to her lips.

Ryan frowned. "She seems to be doing fine."

"Okay. Tell me if that changes, and I'll talk to Joe about letting her off the hook."

He'd what? Jess took in a deep breath, ready to let her brother know exactly what she thought about that idea. Let her off the hook. Sheesh. Like she's some kind of child who can't handle a competition? A *business* competition? Please. If he had any idea of the kinds of cyber security she spent her off hours dodging . . . no. It was good he had no idea there.

No one needed to know about that. Especially not her brother. Or Ryan.

"Sure, no problem." Ryan shook his head in an exaggerated fashion. Was that supposed to convince her he wasn't going to tattle on her? She didn't buy it for a second. "See you when I get home. Enjoy the quiet."

"Yeah. Later, man." The click of the call ending left the inside of the car in silence.

Jess shifted in her seat and pinned Ryan with a glare. "Gee. If it's all too much for my pretty little head, are you going to tell Joe to find you someone else? Maybe Marlene? Or, I know. Rosa. She'd *love* the chance to spend a lot of time with you. I bet her shirts would get even more revealing if she knew she had a reason to drape herself over your shoulder."

He cleared his throat. "Come on, Jess. He's just looking out for you. Chris loves you."

"Mmmhmm." It was going to be time to have another chat with her brother soon, that much was obvious.

"I'm not going to tell him you can't handle this. You know that, right? You're a huge asset to the division, and I don't think anyone was surprised when you ended up part of this competition." Ryan reached over and touched her hand. "I'm serious."

Jess ignored the warmth spreading up her arm from his fingers the same way she'd been ignoring it since she was seventeen. He didn't mean anything by it. He never did. It was just his way of making sure she paid attention. Ryan was a touchy-feely guy. It was part of the reason Marlene and Rosa were convinced they could get him to look their way if they tried hard enough for long enough.

He sighed. "I'm sorry. I'll tell him to butt out."

"You will?" Jess straightened and studied his profile.

Ryan zipped past a car to snag a parking spot near enough to the burger joint that they could walk without freezing. "Sure. It's hard for him—and okay, for me, too, sometimes—to remember you're a grown woman who doesn't need anyone looking out for her."

"I didn't say that." She pushed the button to release her seatbelt.

"You kind of did." He waited for a car to pass before pushing open his door and hopping down from the SUV.

Jess followed suit. She stuffed her hands in her pockets and fell into step beside Ryan. "I don't—it's just maybe you could figure out a way to remember that I'm not a little kid. I appreciate your concern—both of you—and I like knowing you've got my back. But I'm not a baby."

"No, you're really not."

Jess's breath caught as something sparked in his eyes. It was gone before she could be sure—but was it possible that it was appreciation of her as a woman? Not that it would matter. Christopher would shut down anything that tried to happen before it had a chance. As far as her big brother was concerned, no one was good enough for his baby sister.

Not even his oldest, dearest friend.

Stop dwelling on the impossible, girl. She bumped his hip as they walked, and his steps skittered as he tripped. "Just keep that in mind."

He laughed and shoved her gently. "It might be easier if you stopped acting like one all the time."

Jess smiled as the tightness around her heart loosened. She and Ryan were friends. It was enough.

She'd be a fool to ruin their friendship.

Especially when he didn't feel the same way.

And it would make things awkward on so many levels.

Jess took a breath and fortified the walls around her heart with a stern mental reminder. "You're going to share your fries with me, right?"

Ryan snorted. "Just get your own."

"I don't want a whole order."

"You always say that, and then you eat more than half of mine."

"More than half isn't the same thing as all."

He glowered at her. "Fine. But I'm ordering a large and you're paying the difference."

She opened her mouth to object, then shrugged. "Yeah, all right."

He bumped her fist. "Deal. Come on, I'm starving."

Jess nodded and watched him tug open the door to the hamburger joint. She was starving too. But some appetites weren't going to get appeased.

Not by Ryan.

Jess started up Tor on her computer, then drummed her fingers on her desk. She fought the urge to look over her shoulder. There was no one else here—she lived alone —but still. What she was doing wasn't *technically* illegal, but it was frowned on.

Plus, she couldn't guarantee there wouldn't be a need to cross a few of the stricter lines to get all the information she needed.

It was for a good cause. A necessary one. And law enforcement couldn't cross the lines—they were hampered by them, which meant in this case, the bad guys won and the innocent suffered.

What she was doing would help people.

Jess nodded and took a deep breath. She added a few of her own homegrown anonymity measures to the mix. There was no point in making it easy for anyone looking for ShadowWarrior to trace it back to her. And there were a lot of reasons to make it as close to impossible as she could. Most of those reasons related back to the lines that had to be crossed here and there to make a difference.

That should do it.

Now for the fun part.

Jess grinned and got to work.

She'd been watching this group for close to three months. It was their own fault they'd gotten on her radar. She hadn't been looking—she really had been trying to stick to the straight and narrow. Her job in the cyber security division helped. The work she did shoring up access holes and tracing attacks kept her interested and active, and their clients were the good guys. Joe Robinson made sure of that.

Hmm. That was something that should go into their five-year plan. They needed to continue to vet potential clients to ensure they weren't enabling shady business. Joe's businesses all had a squeaky-clean reputation. They needed to keep that.

And still. When traffickers were stupid enough to launch a half-hearted denial-of-service attack on the feds and attempt to take down their servers? They were just *asking* for a white hat to take them out. In fact, the day the news hit about the attempted DDoS, the white-hat hackers—the good guys of the hacking world—had started forming hunting parties. She didn't participate in those. Mostly because she wasn't a team player, but also? The quickest way to get caught was to align with the wrong people, and in the world of the anonymous, it was a challenge to figure out whom to trust.

They were looking for her.

It wasn't paranoia when she knew it was the truth. The white hats wanted to know who she was, because she didn't play nice. The feds were worried about those crossed lines. And that was why she had layers of identities and false trails to protect the ShadowWarrior identity.

Yikes! That was close. Someone had set a sneaky trap—they were good. Not as good as Jess, but close.

She pushed the last thoughts of anything other than the

hunt from her mind as she dug into the target server. There were three locations that were easy to find—those had to be bait. She shuttled the information over. She'd still provide it, but she was going to recommend the feds ignore it. Or maybe they could find a way to use it as a ruse to keep the bad guys complacent. That was well beyond her interest and her pay grade.

She didn't want to be the one making the bust. Jess just wanted to make sure the men and women responsible for the crimes were brought to justice. Thankfully, anonymous tips that panned out were acceptable in a court of law.

Aha. There. She dug a little deeper and finally unlocked access to the real data mother lode. Sixteen locations. Much more like what she expected. Including a fancy hotel in the middle of DC. Evil didn't only live in the sketchy, run-down places.

What was that? She scrolled back to another encrypted folder. And paused. Her gaze darted over to the timer she kept running. She was cutting it close.

And yet.

She snagged the folder. It'd be better to decrypt onsite, if she could. Her first attempts to break the encryption failed.

Now what?

She took the information she had and set it up as a message to the Special Agent who actually seemed invested in following up on the information Jess gave. Jess had no delusion that the woman wasn't also just as invested in figuring out who Jess was, though.

Crossed lines.

If it came to it, she'd do the time.

The work she did was important. And if the feds did their job, there would be boys and girls rescued and returned home before too much longer. Before this organization had a chance to move them. Again.

Jess double-checked that the message would appear to have originated within the traffickers' network, hit Send, and started the tedious process of backing out of the system without leaving a trail.

To be safe, she spent another fifteen minutes sliding through security on other servers and backing out of them. If there was a trail, it needed to be confusing. And then it needed to fade away before it could be traced back.

Grinning, Jess shut down her machine and stood. She stretched her arms over her head and twisted from side to side. Her muscles practically wept with relief. She'd been sitting at her computer for just under three hours. That, in itself, wasn't a lot. The added tension that came from sneaking was always evident in her muscles and joints when she finished a hacking session.

It probably didn't help that it was nearly two in the morning, on a work night, after spending a solid nine hours in her cube working problems for pay.

"Time for bed."

Jess chuckled quietly as she moved around her condo switching off lights and checking locks. She paused to run a hand down the back of her sleeping cat. Meowth opened one eye and studied her for a moment. What did the cat see? Whatever it was, it must not have bothered the fluffy gray Persian, because he snuggled tighter in his cat bed and watched her.

"Night, baby." Jess detoured into the kitchen for a glass of water. She took the drink over to the tiny window looking out on the matching condo building that speared into the sky beside hers. They were all part of the same association, with shared amenities and scheduled social activities designed to make it feel less like living in an anonymous hive and more like there was a chance to know the neighbors. She didn't care about any of that. In many ways, it was nice to be on the outside, looking in. If people looked too closely, they might see more than she wanted.

Ryan did.

Jess frowned and drained the water. She wasn't thinking about Ryan. She'd made it through all of the day at work without obsessing over every last look he'd sent her way while they'd eaten burgers and fries.

They'd kept it casual. Friendly.

Because that was what it was. That was *all* it was. It was all it ever could be.

She'd just keep repeating that to herself until she believed it. Or until Ryan found a girl, fell in love, and married her. Surely that would help Jess finally get over him.

Except just thinking about it cracked her heart. "Jerk. Too stupid to see what's right there, in front of his eyes. And if he did look, my dumb brother would slug him and tell him to choose. Ry would choose Chris's friendship. He has to. Because that's who he is. No one cares where that leaves me."

Meowth padded into the kitchen and sat at her feet, back ramrod straight. He let out a quiet mew.

"Right? I don't know why I spend so much time thinking about him, either. Seven years, buddy." Jess set her glass in the sink and bent to scoop up her cat. She nuzzled her face in his fur and sighed. "I ought to find someone else. Even though neither Ry nor Chris would approve. I guess in their minds, I'm just supposed to stay the little kid who chased after them on her bike, begging to be included. But I'm not that girl anymore. I can do stuff."

Meowth purred and head-butted her shoulder.

"Tonight? That was good work. And if the records I skimmed are accurate, more than a hundred teens, some of whom I recognize from the missing and endangered lists." She bit her lip. Would the feds act fast enough to rescue them? "They're going to have to do their part. I'm going to have to trust that God is going to take it from here. Even if I don't understand why He didn't step in before all this happened."

Meowth grumbled in the back of his throat.

"Oh, I know. God doesn't micromanage the world, and sin is a thing—just seems like the people who are bent on doing true evil ought to get thwapped before they have the chance to ruin so many lives. It'd help out God's image, if nothing else. Like, He could use better PR. The whole bad things happen to good people has kept more than one person I know from believing in Jesus." Truth be told, it was something she wrestled with. A lot. But she wasn't going to say it aloud. Not even to her cat. Some things were better kept to inside voices. Or ignored.

"I'm doing a lot of that lately, aren't I?" Jess kissed the top of her cat's head and strode toward her bedroom.

Meowth leapt from her arms to the foot of the bed, where he curled back into a fluffy ball, his head tucked under his tail.

Her cat had the right idea. Eat, sleep, play, and leave the rest of the worrying to someone else. She could do that now. At least for a little while.

If only Ryan . . . no. *Just stop, Jess.*

She rubbed over her heart. She'd been getting along just fine for seven years. There was no reason anything had to change now.

～

"I THINK THAT WENT WELL, don't you?" Ryan checked over his shoulder to make sure they were clear of anyone who could overhear. "Tyler seemed to like our five-year plan, right?"

"He seemed like it, sure." Jess smiled and pushed the button for the elevator. "You weren't really worried, were you?"

He shrugged. Truthfully, maybe a little. Jess had given them a lot of ideas—and they seemed good on the surface, but it wasn't as if either of them had the business degrees that would say for sure one way or the other. He held up a hand with fingers spaced an inch apart. "This much, I guess?"

"Oh ye of little faith."

He snorted. "You were one hundred percent confident?"

"Yeah, sure. Why not? We had good ideas. Some are unique, some aren't. We researched them, so it's not like anything was completely out of left field. And I think Tyler would have said something when we checked in with the draft last week if there had been something majorly off. Don't you?"

"Definitely." Tyler didn't pull punches. His lips twitched. "After the way he went at Christopher and Stephanie for trying to just divide the work? He would totally have said if we were heading the wrong direction."

"Oh, man. Poor Chris. Although, I don't actually have a problem with Stephanie like he does, so . . ."

"You don't have to work with her."

Jess tilted her head to the side. "And you have?"

Well, no. But he heard all the stories that Christopher brought home. Of course, he also heard here and there how she was handling Rick and meeting deadlines despite the guy's attempts to sabotage everything. So she probably wasn't as bad as Chris made out. If Ryan had to guess, there was an element of protesting too much going on with his roomie when it came to Stephanie. But he wasn't going to meddle in that at all.

The very last thing Ryan needed was to be asked about his own love life. He could only dodge the conversation so many times before he had to admit that he had a crush on his best friend's sister. If he could, Ryan was going to put that off long enough that the feelings went away.

"What's taking the elevator so long?" Jess stabbed the button again.

"Don't know. They get slow sometimes."

Jess checked her watch and frowned. "Yeah, well I told Shupe I'd help him with the firewall settings. I guess I'm taking the stairs. You coming?"

Ryan shook his head. "I'll wait. I don't have anything urgent."

Jess laughed. "I heard you've started working out. I thought maybe you'd get into the stairs thing with me, too."

"I went to the gym to avoid barging in on your brother and Stephanie's work time." It hadn't been that bad. He'd walked on the treadmill for an hour. It had been slow—leisurely, even— but it had left him alert and focused.

It was his own fault that his alert, focused thoughts had drifted to Jess.

"Yeah, well, I'm going to work out tonight, if you're interested in making it a weekly thing. I'd love the company. Usually it's deserted down there."

"I'll keep it in mind." His heart was already speeding up. Time alone with Jess that wasn't work related? Yes, please. He'd text Chris and see if he and Stephanie were planning on meeting in their apartment again. If they were, maybe he'd go ahead and swing down to the gym after all. "What time? Just in case."

"Maybe seven?" She shot him a grin as she grabbed the door handle for the stairs. "See you around."

"Yeah, bye." There was no way she'd heard him. Whatever. They'd meet up in the gym, and maybe this would be the push he needed to actually enjoy exercise. Desk jobs weren't known for their ability to keep a guy fit. Oh, sure, Ryan still had that magic metabolism he'd had since high school, but he could look at his dad and see the writing on the wall. If he didn't want to end up toting a seven-month pregnancy sized belly around with him at forty like his dad had, Ryan was going to need to figure out some kind of exercise that he enjoyed enough to actually do.

Exercising with Jess seemed like it might just be the thing.

"Ryan Foster?"

He turned, frowning slightly as his gaze landed on the pair of men in dark, off-the-rack suits. "That's me. Can I help you?"

"I'm Special Agent Mosby with the FBI. Is there a place we could talk?"

Ryan bit back a sigh. What had Jess done now? And more importantly, did they *know* it was her? Or did they just suspect it? "Sure, my office?"

The elevator finally arrived. Ryan gestured toward it.

"That will be fine."

Ryan's mind raced as they stepped into the elevator and descended to the floor occupied by the cyber division. The best thing to do—the way he always tried to play it—was to act curious and uninformed. Let them talk, promise to think about it, and absolutely never mention or even think about Jess.

When they got to his office, Ryan took the seat behind his desk and gestured to the two visitor chairs.

Special Agent Mosby shut the door.

Ryan fought the urge to stiffen. Why did everything seem ominous when the FBI was around? "So. How can I help you? I know Cyber has a few contracts with the FBI, but I don't have any direct participation."

The men sat and exchanged a glance. Mosby folded his hands in his lap. "We're in the process of investigating some serious incursions perpetrated by an individual using the name ShadowWarrior."

Ryan must have looked confused, because Mosby paused and exchanged another glance with his yet-to-be-introduced counterpart.

The other man spoke. "You're unfamiliar with this handle?"

"I am. It sounds like something out of a comic book. You're serious?"

"Very." Back to Mosby. At least the guy seemed to regroup quickly. "You know your employee, Jessica Ward, has been associated with hacking in her past?"

Here Ryan needed to tread carefully. "It's my understanding that there were several unproven allegations, yes."

"You sound like her attorney." Mosby shook his head and shot Ryan a look that clearly said, "Get real." Even if he didn't say the words. "Just because the evidence was insufficient to convince a jury doesn't mean the government is unsure of the truth of the situation."

"I'm not the government, so I've always thought the outcome of the trial was sufficient for any opinions that I needed to form." Ryan swallowed. He'd had to go to bat with Joe, as had Christopher, when they'd recommended hiring Jess. As it was, her history got brought up with every new client, and she wasn't able to hold a security clearance. It had probably cost them a contract here or there, but the clients who took the chance recognized that Jess was an incredible asset to the team. Ryan agreed. "Is there evidence connecting this SpiderWarrior to Jessica?"

"*Shadow*Warrior." Mosby's lips thinned as he pressed them together. His whole face looked pinched. "Not at this time."

"I see." And he did. They were fishing. "What was it you were hoping to accomplish here?"

"We'd like to speak to Ms. Ward."

His first instinct was to say no. Would that make her look guilty though? Would it implicate him? The truth was, he didn't know anything about a ShadowWarrior. He also didn't know anything about Jess still hacking. Oh, he suspected she did. She was big on keeping her hand in things that she enjoyed. But suspecting wasn't the same as knowing. Besides, when would she have time? Especially now with the company contest. "She's working on a time-sensitive deliverable right now. Let me give her a call and see if she can spare you a moment."

"We can go to her." Mosby started to rise.

"I think you'll be more comfortable here. In the privacy of my office. We wouldn't want anyone to get the wrong idea."

"What wrong idea is that?" Mosby cocked his head to the side.

"I could be wrong. I'm not a lawyer, but I do think public false accusations are considered libel. Or is it slander? I can never keep the two straight. Still. It's one of them, I'm pretty sure." Ryan offered a sharp, toothy grin and reached for the handset of his desk phone without breaking eye contact.

Mosby sank back into his chair, his expression tightening.

Ryan tapped Jess's extension and waited as it rang. Her cube was near Shupe's. If she was still there, she should hear her phone.

She answered, slightly out of breath. "Jess Ward."

"Hi, it's Ryan. I have two gentlemen from the FBI who'd like to speak to you in my office. Are you available?"

Jess's intake of breath was sharp. "Um. Yeah. Give me five?"

"Soon as you can. Thanks." Ryan set the phone back in its cradle. "She'll be here in a few minutes. I'm sure you have other people who have been accused of wrongdoing but never convicted to speak to as well."

"Your loyalty is admirable, but misplaced." The man who was not Mosby leaned forward as he spoke. "Jessica Ward isn't some do-gooder saving the world."

Ryan lifted his brows. "No. She's an exemplary employee who's able to solve hard problems. Her clients love her speedy work, attention to detail, and the fact that she keeps their systems safe and secure."

"Haven't you ever wondered why?" Mosby's face relaxed into a sympathetic frown. "It takes a thief to catch one."

"I've heard the phrase." Ryan shrugged. "But I never really considered it accurate. After all, that would mean everyone in law enforcement—or at least the ones who are good at their jobs —is also crooked."

Not-Mosby's lips twitched.

Well, at least someone had a sense of humor. Or part of one. Ryan searched around for something else to talk about while they waited for Jess. Thankfully, there was a knock at the door before he had to come up with something to break the silence. "Come in."

Jess pushed the door open, a quizzical smile on her face. "You said there were people to see me?"

"Jess, this is Agent Mosby from the FBI and his friend." Ryan gestured to the two men.

"*Special* Agent Mosby." He stood and pointed to his chair. "We'd like to ask you some questions."

"I see. Do I need my attorney?" Jess's eyebrows hiked up into her hairline.

"Not unless you have something to hide."

Jess laughed so hard she had to bend over and catch her breath. She held up a finger as she worked to stave off the giggles. Finally, she cleared her throat and shook her head. "Oh, man. You don't think I'm going to fall for that again, do you? Last time I believed you people when you said that, I ended up on trial for crimes I didn't commit. Crimes I was cleared of, as you well know. And yet, somehow, despite my innocence, every time you people get a wild hair, you're showing up here or at my home to nag me. So why don't you just tell me what you think it is I've done now, and I'll decide if I need to call my attorney."

"Ms. Ward. Have a seat." Mosby gestured to the chair a second time.

"No thank you."

Ryan bit the inside of his lip. Was this really the best way to handle it? It sure wasn't what he'd do, but then, he hadn't spent six months of his life on trial like Jess had. For all he knew, this is exactly what her attorney had counseled her to do if—well, when—they had to know it was when—the feds showed up again.

Mosby scowled. "Are you the hacker operating under the handle *ShadowWarrior*?"

"No. Is that all?" Jess crossed her arms.

"Would you tell us if you were?" The other man spoke from where he sat, seemingly relaxed and unfazed by the sparks that flew between Jess and Mosby.

"I don't make a habit of lying." Jess's fists clenched. "Is there anything else?"

"What do you know about—" Mosby broke off when the other man stood and touched his arm.

"We'll be in touch."

Mosby's head whipped around and he stared at his colleague. Anger simmered in his eyes.

Would it come to blows? From where Ryan was sitting, it certainly seemed possible.

After a moment, Mosby relaxed and gave a curt nod. "Thank you for your time."

"Sorry we couldn't be more help." Ryan stood and slid around the desk. He walked to the office door, beating Mosby there, and opened it for the men from the FBI. "Have a good day. I hope you catch your man."

"Oh, we will." Mosby turned and stared over his shoulder at Jess. "Eventually."

Jess offered a fake, bright smile.

Ryan closed the door behind the departing men and sagged against it. "What are you up to, Jess?"

4

Jess ran full out, her feet pounding on the treadmill. Each slap of her sneakers she imagined as a fist slamming into the face of one of the men from the FBI. Or Ryan.

What am I up to? Nothing. That's what. Of course, Ryan didn't believe her. He'd pushed, a little, but she hadn't said anything. Instead, she'd slid her hands along the edge of his desk and under the cushion of his office chairs until she'd found the listening device they'd left for him.

It hadn't been as satisfying as she'd expected to show it to Ryan before smashing it under her heel.

In fact, knowing him as well as she did, he probably considered the fact that they'd been willing to plant anything in his office as a confirmation that she'd done something wrong.

Typical.

Jess punched the button to increase the speed of her run.

Sweat ran through her hair and down her back. She was soaked with it. And still she couldn't shake her anger.

Mosby. He'd had it out for her since the very beginning. He hadn't known she was ShadowWarrior. If Mosby had even the tiniest shred of circumstantial evidence that tied something to Jess, she would've been handcuffed and in the back of their car the moment they were on the premises.

So they'd been fishing.

What had Ryan told them?

She fought against the stab of disappointment that he'd assumed—and okay, fine, he'd assumed rightly—that she was doing something. But it was good! After Mosby's visit, she'd risked a quick peek at her chosen contact's activity, and the woman was chasing the leads, gathering the evidence, and building a case. Those kids were going to get home safely in the next week, provided no one like Special Agent Mosby blew it.

Jess frowned. Was it possible Mosby was crooked? Not just bumbling and sour because of a misplaced vendetta? That would complicate things. And it bore looking into. She'd just have to be extra careful. Knowing Mosby, he'd have traps set.

"Whoa." Ryan peered up at her. "You okay?"

Jess jolted as his arrival jarred her out of her thoughts. "Fine. I did say I was working out."

"True. This just seems a little extra."

"Like you'd know." Okay, maybe that was excessive. Ryan wasn't the bad guy here. Probably. He wasn't exactly the good one, either. Wasn't he supposed to be on her side? They were friends. Had been forever, hadn't they? Even though he was Chris's friend first, he was still hers, too. "You just watching or did you plan to work out too?"

"I'm trying to decide if I need to wait. In case I need to call an ambulance."

Jess rolled her eyes, but she tapped the button to lower the speed of the treadmill. "Better?"

"Sure."

"Oh, that was convincing." She took a deep breath, now that she could. Maybe running flat out wasn't the best idea after all.

"What's your problem? You're not the one the FBI is gunning for."

"No. But they're hounding my friend. Am I allowed to be annoyed by that?" Ryan stepped onto the treadmill beside her and tapped the button until he was moving at a steady walk. "I'm sorry I couldn't figure out a way to get them to go without bugging you."

Her mouth dropped open.

"What? You thought I wanted them there? That I believed them?" He shook his head. "Nice."

"Oh, please. With your whole 'what are you up to, Jess?' like I'm some kind of kid that got caught out after curfew." A tiny niggle of guilt clawed at her. She *was* ShadowWarrior. She *was* out there doing things she knew Ryan and Chris wouldn't approve of. Well, the hacking part. Both of them would agree that helping shut down trafficking was a good thing. Didn't the ends ever justify the means?

"I'm sorry. That wasn't what I meant. I don't want you to get caught up in something that ruins the amazing life you have ahead of you. I mean, come on. You're going to end up running the Cyber division."

Jess snorted and slowed her treadmill another few notches. "Please. You're going to win this. And I'm fine with that. I'm fine helping you do that. They need a straight arrow in charge of something like cyber—I definitely don't qualify there."

"Innocent, remember?" Ryan glanced at her. What was that in his eyes? Concern, sure, but what else lurked in there?

"Technically, you mean not guilty. It isn't quite the same thing. And there will always be people like Mosby who are convinced the jury got it wrong." Mostly, they had. She had hacked the systems. She hadn't stolen the money or the secrets, but she also hadn't paid enough attention to what she was doing and how, so others had taken advantage and followed the trail.

She'd made it possible, even if she hadn't actually done the crime. Was that happening now, too?

No. Jess was careful now—too careful, maybe. If that was a thing.

"You didn't steal money, Jess. Or secrets. No one who knows you believes you're capable of doing any of the things they charged you with."

She smiled and stopped the machine. "But you don't believe I didn't hack the servers."

"I believe you're capable of hacking them. I believe you're capable of compromising any system that you're interested in compromising. You're just that good. But I also know—not believe, mind you, know. With one hundred percent certainty. If you hacked into something, it wouldn't be so you could personally gain."

Jess stepped off the treadmill and crossed to the alcohol wipes provided by the gym. She came back and cleaned the machine. Finished, she snagged her towel and covered her face. What did it mean that Ryan found exactly the words she needed to hear? Just like he always did.

It meant he was her brother's best friend and had known her too long.

She scrubbed her face and neck, drying some of the sweat before moving to the free weights. She picked up a set of ten-pound hand weights and faced the mirror as she began slow, controlled bicep curls. "Thank you."

"You're welcome." He puffed a little as he walked. "I think you should tell Christopher."

"No. Way." That was non-negotiable. She looked up and met his gaze in the mirror. "You can't, either."

"Jess." Ryan frowned. "He's going to find out. The freaking FBI was in the building. What do you think he's going to assume?"

That was true. Christopher had zero intention of giving her the benefit of the doubt when it came to the trouble she'd been in. "I'll think about it. What did Mosby ask you?"

Ryan shrugged. "Basically, the same thing. I guess this ShadowWarrior guy is giving them a headache."

"He said that?"

"Well, no. I just assumed. I mean—why else would they be asking about him?"

Jess shook her head and switched to her triceps. It was a good question. She might be able to disguise her location, but she'd created the identity specifically to send information to her contact at the FBI. So of course Mosby could find out that such a handle existed. But did he have the skills to do any tracing? How had he ended up in Ryan's office looking for her?

"I don't get the idea Mosby's your biggest fan." Ryan grinned.

"Yeah, he was at the trial and super unhappy when I didn't get convicted." She set the weights down and shook out her arms. "So, what, you got back to your office and they were there waiting for you?"

"No. They showed up right after you hit the stairs so you wouldn't be late for Shupe."

Jess bit her lip. They'd been up on the executive floor? Why would they do that? That had to mean they'd been talking to Joe. Or Tyler. Maybe both Joe and Tyler? Ugh. Her stomach knotted. Was her job in jeopardy? "I think I need you to run this whole thing from the top."

"Why? They left."

"Ry. Come on. I need to know if I should get in touch with my lawyer, after all." She didn't want to do that. She really, *really* didn't want to do that. But she wouldn't be caught off guard by these guys again. Not if she could help it.

"Okay." Ryan stopped the treadmill and stepped off. "But what if we eat ice cream while I talk."

"Ice cream." Jess frowned at him. On the other hand, it did sound good. Today was not her day for dessert. And yet, Ryan wasn't a big sweet eater. "Yeah, all right. I have rocky road in my freezer."

He grinned. "Figured you would."

"You're going to wipe that down, right?" Jess nodded toward the treadmill. She cleaned the weights and set them back on their rack.

Ryan rolled his eyes but cleaned the treadmill. "I hardly touched the thing. Plus, I'm not the one who was sweating all over the place."

"It's true, you weren't. Which begs the question, why were you pretending to work out again?"

He bristled. "I'll have you know I was not pretending anything. And you're the one who invited me down here. Or did you forget?"

"I didn't. I just thought—" Jess snapped her mouth closed on the rest of that sentence. She'd thought Ryan was on the side of the FBI agents. That he assumed she was guilty. She was wrong.

"You thought?" Ryan pressed the button for the elevator.

"Never mind." She stepped into the elevator and tapped the button for her floor. Chris and Ryan were three floors lower. Of course they had a bigger place with better views, but they also had a higher combined paycheck. She made it work on her own. Barely. "What do you think will be the next big project for this contest?"

"I guess we'll find out February first." Ryan shrugged. "I'm not worried. We make a good team."

She nodded.

The elevator stopped on her floor, and they got off. They made their way through the halls in silence. At her door, Jess fished the lanyard that held her keys out from under her T-shirt and unlocked the deadbolts.

Meowth came running, chatting away in his rumbly cat way about whatever had annoyed him while she was gone.

Jess chuckled and scooped him up. "Hey, buddy."

Ryan reached over to ruffle the cat's ears. "Hey, tubbo."

"Hey. He's beautiful and sleek just like he should be." Jess kicked the door closed behind them. "Can you turn the locks?"

"Sleek? On what planet?" Ryan flipped the knobs on the three deadbolts Jess had on her front door.

"Any planet. He's fluffy, is all. Persians are supposed to be."

Ryan rolled his eyes, but they were full of laughter.

Jess stopped herself from defending Meowth again and pointed at Ryan. "You're egging me on."

"You think?" He grinned. "Ice cream, I beg you. Before I die."

"Oh yeah, I'm sure fifteen minutes of strolling is going to kill you." Jess set the cat down and went into the kitchen. She washed her hands before getting down two bowls and spoons, and digging through the freezer for the rocky road.

Ryan leaned against the island and watched her scoop. "Don't be stingy."

"When am I ever?" Jess dug into the carton, her mouth watering. "Can I ask you a hypothetical question?"

He sighed. "Why am I terrified?"

"Yes or no, man?" She dropped another scoop into the bowl and pushed it toward Ryan before beginning to scoop her own treat.

"Hit me." Ryan dipped into the ice cream and closed his eyes as he took the first bite.

For just one moment, Jess let herself imagine what it would feel like to have his lips moving against hers. Would he enjoy it as much as he seemed to relish the cold, creamy treat?

"Earth to Jess. What's the question?"

She blinked and focused back down on her dessert. She cleared her throat. "Hypothetically speaking, would it be a good idea or a bad idea to do some digging to see if I could figure out who this ShadowWarrior guy is? I mean, if I got in touch with some of the white hats, I might be able to suss it out."

"Just no. Absolutely not. Negative." He put his spoon into his bowl and leaned forward until their noses nearly touched. "I'm serious. Leave it be."

"But—"

"No." He leaned back and returned to his ice cream. "I know you're not stupid. Why would you even consider it?"

"Because maybe if they had the right person to bother, they'd finally leave me alone. Is that so much to ask?" Jess dug into her ice cream. So much for that idea. She'd had someone in mind to pin it on, too. It wasn't as if ShadowWarrior had done anything terrible. Crossed a few lines, fine, but a good attorney would be able to get the guy off. Look at the good that was done! And in the white-hat world? He'd be a legend. Really, it was almost like doing him a huge favor.

"No. It's not." Ryan reached over and clasped her hand. "It's not fair, and I'm sorry that it's happening. But you need to stay out of it. Far, far out of it so there's no possible way for Mosby to drag you into even the fringes. You understand that he's gunning for you, right?"

Jess nodded. She couldn't speak if she tried. She could blame the cold—ice cream freezing vocal chords was a thing, right? Who was she trying to kid? It was Ryan. Still holding her hand and getting her hopes up, even though he had no idea. "If I tell you something, do you promise not to get mad?"

He closed his eyes. "Oh, Jess."

"I didn't do anything wrong! And I sent information on busting up a trafficking ring. Does that count for anything? Anything at all?"

He squeezed her hand. "Of course it does. But you knew they were watching you before today. Why would you risk it?"

"I don't think he knows anything. He just hates me." Jess shrugged and studied Ryan. "Do you trust me?"

"You know I do."

"Let me show you."

He bit his lip. "It'd mean I'm in this with you. All the way. If you go down, I go with you."

"I'm not asking for that."

"I know. I am."

She blinked. He'd do that? "I can't let you—"

"Non-negotiable."

Gosh, she'd forgotten how stubborn he could be. "Fine. As long as you promise you'll never tell Chris."

"Oh, that's a deal. And if he finds out, I'm going to be praying we get sent to jail for a long, long time."

Jess laughed. Ryan wasn't wrong, though. There were a lot of things for Chris to find out that would be better off staying secret until she and Ryan were out of reach.

THE NEXT TWO weeks were a surreal blur. When he'd agreed to see what Jess was up to, Ryan hadn't known what to expect. But the risks she took digging into the servers of criminals were so far beyond anything he'd anticipated, he'd basically spent the evening—and the days since—shaking his head.

There was hardly any mention in the media of the trafficking bust when it went down.

Jess poked her head into his office. "Did you see the article I sent you?"

"Yeah. That's it?" Ryan frowned at his computer monitor before standing and snagging a notepad off his desk. "I mean, a hundred and twelve girls. You'd think that would be more than a blip you have to dig for."

Jess shrugged. "You'd think, but you'd be wrong. It's an indication of the scope of the problem."

Why wasn't there more information out there about this? Oh, sure, he saw the posts on social media here and there—usually on some kind of awareness day—and then it all faded into nothing. But the problem didn't go away, just people's recognition of it. "I'm proud of you."

Jess's cheeks pinked. She looked away. "It's a drop in the bucket."

"It's better than nothing, though. It made a difference to those kids. Their families." Ryan studied her, annoyed at his wayward heart that practically begged him to reach out and draw her close. She wouldn't go for that—his best friend would be livid, too. Both were good reasons to avoid making his feelings known. He could deal. "Ready for the meeting?"

"I guess. I keep waiting for the FBI to pop out from behind a plant."

He chuckled. Hopefully it wouldn't sound as forced to her as it felt.

"You're not worried?" She glanced up at him as they reached the door to the stairwell.

Ryan gestured for her to go first and fell into step beside her, climbing up to the executive level for the contest conference with Tyler. He didn't know how to answer. He was worried, but he was trying not to be. It wouldn't change anything, and the Bible was pretty clear about the fact that believers weren't supposed to live their lives driven by fear and anxiety. But he was also having a hard time reconciling that with the fact that some of the lines Jess crossed digging for this information had pushed her efforts outside the law. And that wasn't what Jesus wanted, either.

Where was the line? Missionaries smuggled Bibles into countries where it was illegal to preach the gospel and believe in

Jesus. Was that wrong? Or was God okay with a believer doing good things—things that furthered the Kingdom—even if put them outside man's law?

"That's a lot of silence. You *are* worried." Jess bit her lip. "I shouldn't have dragged you into this."

Ryan grabbed her hand and tugged her to a stop. He looked around. The stairwell was empty as far as he could see, but he kept his voice low. "We're in this together. I mean that. I don't regret it at all. I have some things I'm praying about, but right now? So far? I don't have answers."

Jess nodded. "I understand that. You need to figure that out for yourself. I can justify it—but maybe you can't."

"It's less about me and more about whether or not I should." He made himself let go of her hand, even though everything in him craved the touch. "Does that make sense?"

"It does." Jess rubbed his arm before reaching for the stairwell door. "You can walk away. I won't blame you."

"I don't think I can, actually."

Jess cocked her head to the side and studied him.

He shook his head. "Maybe we can talk later."

"Okay." She turned and strode to the conference room.

What had he done? He knew what he *wanted* to talk to her about later, but it was a bad idea. Terrible, even. What if she said no?

What if she said yes?

Ryan followed her, at a distance, into the conference room. His gaze landed on his best friend. Everything in him seemed to constrict. Chris would be so angry if he had even an inkling of an idea about the sorts of thoughts Ryan had when it came to Jess.

What if Jess didn't feel the same way?

Except she had to. Didn't she? It sure seemed like she did. Or at least that she wasn't completely opposed to the idea.

Or maybe he was delusional, and she just liked having someone to share her secret with.

Ryan didn't catch a lot of what Tyler said in the meeting. How much of it really mattered? They'd get an email with the specifications of their next challenge—and the fact that it was Valentine's Day themed when he couldn't get his brain off the idea that he was falling in love with his best friend's sister? That was either amazing or terrible.

Maybe it was amazingly terrible.

Jess's elbow jabbed his ribs.

"What?" He jolted and glanced around. Everyone was leaving.

"Where'd you go?" Her eyes danced with laughter.

"Sorry. I caught the gist. Love, right?"

She shook her head. "Love your *job*. And also? There's something going on with Stephanie and Chris."

"Going on? No way. They're working together the same as you and me."

Jess lifted her eyebrows.

Ryan wanted to hunch his shoulders, but fought to keep them straight. "I'm serious. If Chris was thinking of Stephanie that way, he would've said something to me."

"You sure?"

Guilt snaked through Ryan's belly. Normally, he would be absolutely sure. But lately? He'd been avoiding any sort of room-mate conversation, because he was terrified something would slip out that told his best friend about the feelings he was having for Jess.

Ryan really didn't want to have to find a new place to live.

"I mean, kinda?"

Jess nodded. "Which translates to no. Maybe you and I aren't the only people who need to have a conversation."

He was fairly sure his eyes were going to bug out of his head.

She couldn't possibly mean she wanted him to tell her brother about what was going on between them. Not that there was anything going on. So, of course, she didn't want him to say something, because there was nothing to say! "Um."

"Eloquent. Come on. I have work I should be doing. You probably do, too. Maybe tonight we could grab Mexican and figure out how we're going to make the Cyber gang love their jobs even more than they already do."

Ryan laughed as he stood. "It's tricky, for sure."

"Come on. Stairs. They're faster and less crowded. And now that you work out, you want to keep your muscles moving and limber." Jess reached for the door handle.

Ryan cast a longing look toward the elevator. She was probably right, but still. There was something to be said for laziness.

He started down the stairs slightly behind Jess. Her jeans clung in all the right places. So did the black T-shirt she'd layered over a red thermal. Maybe physical fitness wasn't all bad, after all.

Jess glanced back over her shoulder, with a sly smile. "Enjoying the view?"

Ryan's mouth went dry. There was no way to answer that without looking like an idiot. So he just smiled and jogged down the rest of the flight of stairs, leaving her where she'd paused.

Maybe there was something there.

The question was, what did he do about it?

Making a move on Jess? It would either be the best thing he'd ever done. Or the worst.

Was he willing to take the chance?

5

R yan peeked into the oven. The enormous chicken pot pie he'd picked up at Costco was almost ready. The guys should all be arriving soon. He just had to get through the evening without mentioning the fact that he was sinking deeper into love with Jess every day.

Wait. Love?

No. He liked her, sure. They were friends. And yeah, okay, he found her attractive—who wouldn't? But Love? Like capital L, till death do us part, Love? That was impossible.

They hadn't even been on a date.

He crossed the kitchen and grabbed plates out of the cabinet.

"Smells good. Pot pie?" Christopher slipped into the room and leaned on the island. "Anything I can to do help?"

"Yes to the pot pie. No to the help. Unless you want to get drinks. But I figured everyone could just get what they wanted out of the fridge."

"Yep." Christopher didn't move.

Ryan looked over. "What's up?"

"I think Stephanie and I are dating."

"You think? Shouldn't you know?" And wasn't that rich, coming from him? But he couldn't let on that he had any sort of interest in anyone. Christopher would dig that out faster than a dog after a bone.

"After the meeting today, we went to grab coffee and talk about our plan. Of course, we didn't have any ideas—I mean really, this one's dumb. Stephanie was right on when she said she just wants people to come in, do the job, and then leave. I mean, I had to play devil's advocate, but to a large degree? I didn't actually disagree. Who loves their job?"

Ryan raised his hand with a grin. "Jess and I have the opposite problem."

"Yeah? Everyone in Cyber loves their job? You're serious?" Christopher shook his head. "I don't believe it."

"Believe what you want, but I'd be surprised if there was anyone who dreaded coming into work every day. We're a good group and the work is interesting and fun." Ryan drummed his fingers on his leg. "That actually gives me an idea. Can you keep an eye on the pot pie? I'll be right back."

"Where are you going?"

"I just want to run up and talk to Jess. Five minutes, tops." Ryan jogged to the door and was in the hall before Christopher replied. He hit the stairwell with a mental snicker—Jess would be proud of him—and took some of the stairs two at a time. Then he had to stop and breathe heavily with his hands on his knees, but he could leave that bit out. When he was less winded, he hurried up, at a more reasonable pace, to Jess's condo. He banged on her door.

It felt like forever before the locks clicked and her door opened. Confusion covered her face. "Ryan?"

"I have the best idea." He pointed into her living room. "Can I come in?"

"Don't you have Bible study?"

"Yeah, Chris is watching the pot pie. They can start eating, but this won't take long. What if we did a hackathon?"

Jess stepped away from the door and opened it wider.

Ryan took it as an invitation and strode into her condo.

"Where are your shoes?"

He glanced down at his socks and laughed. The bright yellow emojis that danced across his toes weren't something most people saw. "I guess I got so caught up I forgot. Now that you say it, that might be what your brother was yelling at me when I took off."

Jess shook her head, before glancing up.

Their eyes met.

Ryan swallowed and took a step toward her, all thoughts of the hackathon draining away. "Jess."

She held up a hand and closed her eyes. "I know."

"Bad idea?" He took another step closer.

"Probably."

Ryan stepped closer again, until the toes of his socks bumped the bright pink of her toenails. "So is that a no?"

She opened her eyes and sucked in a breath. She pressed her lips together and gave her head the tiniest shake. "No."

Did she mean . . . whatever. She could step back if that was what she needed to do. Ryan's arms snaked out and wrapped around her, pulling her close even as he lowered his mouth to hers. Every intention of keeping it slow, sweet, and simple fled when their lips met. His hands moved to her hair, tangling in the silky strands as his lips feasted on hers.

Her hands slid up his chest and clenched fistfuls of his shirt.

Ryan lost all sense of time and space. There was only Jess.

And him.

And their kiss.

He'd entertained some fanciful dreams of holding and

kissing Jess—and yet those dreams faded in comparison to reality.

Ryan would have sworn he could hear angels singing. Well, let them sing.

Jess nudged him, easing back slightly. "Ry."

"Just a minute." He mumbled against her mouth before reclaiming her lips as they curved.

"Ry." Jess reached up and circled his wrists, giving them a gentle tug before stepping back and blowing out a breath. "Wow."

He blinked, coming back down to earth. "I'm pretty sure I heard angels singing."

"I think that was your cell." The music started again as Jess spoke. She grinned at him and his heart soared.

"Oh." Duh. Ryan reached into his back pocket for his phone and his stomach sank. Christopher.

"You can answer it. Then tell me your idea."

He shook his head and flipped the phone around so she could see the screen.

"Oh." Jess paled. She cleared her throat. "You really need to answer. On your way back down. You've been here fifteen minutes."

"What? No . . ." Ryan frowned at the time on his phone. "Oh, boy."

Jess was already pushing him toward the door. "Go go go."

"But—"

"Go. Hackathon. It's brilliant. I'll figure out what we talked about if he asks me. Just go." She leaned in and pressed a fast kiss on his lips before shoving him out into the hallway and slamming the door in his face.

Ryan scrubbed his hands over his face. The phone started ringing again. He answered as he jogged down the hall. "Sorry. I'm coming. You started eating, right?"

"Yeah, man. Jess okay?"

Ryan fought to keep his voice casual. "Oh, yeah. We just got caught up."

"Well I'm glad someone has a good idea." Bitterness laced Christopher's words. "Anyway, you're going to have to eat while we get started. Aaron needs to leave early."

"I'm almost there." Ryan pushed the stairwell door open on their floor and ended the call. He could do this. Dodge. Get someone else talking. Keep everyone on topic with the Bible study. Then disappear claiming exhaustion.

Because letting on that he'd just spent the best fifteen minutes of his life not talking with Jess was the worst possible thing he could do.

For everyone involved.

JESS LET her mind empty as she ran on the treadmill. Or at least she tried to. Ever since the kiss on Monday night—and oh, boy, what a kiss—it had been the only thing she'd been able to concentrate on.

Who would have thought Ryan had that sort of skill?

She frowned slightly. She'd known him practically her whole life. It wasn't as though he didn't date—he had a reputation for dating a lot, in fact. But she'd also gotten the idea from things Christopher said that the reputation was unearned. Not that she'd hung on every word or anything. But still. Presumably, however many people Ryan had dated, they'd done more than sit around and kiss. Although . . . she could get behind that idea.

But what if . . .

Jess grabbed her water bottle and took a sip as her feet continued to pound away on the three-mile course she'd programmed. Okay, might as well let the thought play out. What if Ryan regretted the kiss?

She'd dated here and there, but really had only had one serious boyfriend. And even then, "serious" had meant more that they spent all their Friday and Saturday nights together playing online sword-fighting games. He'd needed another clan member for the online battles, and Jess had been curious enough to give it a shot. Since she was basically the only person Deke knew in real life rather than online, they'd become a bit of a de facto couple.

The one time he'd kissed her was not an earth-moving scenario.

She fought a shudder at the memory of his clammy and yet somehow still slobbery lips on her cheek and mouth. He'd absolutely missed—and rather than laughing and trying again, he'd tried to play it off like he was trailing kisses across her face. Oh there'd been a trail all right, but it had been like a snail's slime trail, not something romantic and sexy.

"Hey."

Jess jolted, her head whipping to the side at Ryan's voice.

He grinned. "Sorry. Didn't mean to scare you."

She narrowed his eyes. "You did, too. I bet you tiptoed on purpose."

"Hey, it's not my fault you get into your running zone and lose sight of the world outside." He glared at the treadmill beside her before climbing on and starting up the belt. He glanced over at the display on hers and his eyebrows lifted. "You've already run two miles? How long have you been down here?"

"Long enough to run two miles. I don't know, twenty minutes?" Might be closer to fifteen, but why make him feel bad? She wasn't running all out, but she could keep a decent pace for shorter runs. "I was thinking I might train for a marathon."

"Why?" He bumped up the speed until he was walking quickly. "That sounds horrible."

She chuckled. Scratch that off the list of things they could do together. "The Marine Corps marathon is in October every year. It sounds kinda fun."

"I'll take your word for it. But I know people go up and cheer. I'll be there with a huge, embarrassing sign."

Jess's heart melted. "You'd do that?"

"Of course I would. Even before Monday I would've." He cleared his throat. "About that."

Please don't let him be gearing up to say he shouldn't have done it. Please. She fought the urge to cut him off. It was better to know if he regretted it. Wasn't it?

"I wanted to ask if I should apologize."

"I really wish you wouldn't." Her heart hammered in her chest, but now it wasn't from exertion.

"No?" He looked over at her. She met his gaze and willed him to understand the depth of her feelings for him. He smiled. "Okay. Then I guess I have a follow-up question."

"Yeah? What's that?" Her treadmill signaled the end of her program and started to slow.

"Could we do it again sometime soon?"

Was now too soon? Jess considered throwing herself off her treadmill and into his arms, but that was probably only going to end up injuring both of them in ways they'd never be able to explain to her brother. "I'd really like to."

Ryan pumped his fist, lost his footing, and had to jog to keep from tripping completely off his exercise equipment.

Jess laughed.

"Quiet, you. It's not funny."

"Oh, yes, it is. It's hilarious." She wiped down her machine and moved to the free-weight area. "Do you want to come up to my place when we're done here? I had an idea about the hackathon."

"The what?"

Jess shot him a look. "You don't remember why you came over on Monday?"

Ryan shrugged. "I got a little distracted."

"Me, too. And yet, the hackathon is genius. I've put a little time into fleshing out what it would be, and I'm thinking capture the flag. That's by far the most fun—and the easiest to set up on short notice."

"Capture the flag?"

Jess rolled her eyes as she began a set of bicep curls. Sometimes she forgot that Ryan didn't come from the hacking world. Not even the cyber security degree end of things. He'd majored in computer science, but focused on programming. "How did you even end up in Cyber?"

"I'm a good project manager, and I didn't want to keep coding. I understand the lingo, and can usually follow the technical conversations even if I couldn't always do the stuff you talk about."

She considered that a moment before nodding. That was fair. And he'd learned a lot, especially if he'd come up with the idea of a hackathon in the first place. "Okay. So at the hacking conferences, there's always a capture the flag game. Basically, we have teams, and each team has a server with information on it that we need to protect. The goal is to capture the other team's information without being detected while defending your own server at the same time. It's fun!"

"If you say so. What do people like me do?" He continued plodding along on his treadmill.

Oh. Well. Hm. She hadn't actually given that a lot of thought. She frowned and concentrated on raising and lowering her dumbbells. There weren't many layers of management and non-technical support staff in Cyber, but there were enough that they'd need some kind of task. "Psyops."

He blinked. "We're doing psychological warfare as part of a capture the flag game?"

"Sure. People give away all kinds of data on a daily basis without thinking about it. Like those name generators on social media—the funny ones, right? You can get people to give you all their security question answers by promising to let them know what their Santa's Reindeer name is at the end of it."

"Too bad it's not Christmas."

Jess groaned. "Fine, your Cupid name. It's all the same stuff. And people lap it up."

"Not the people who work for us."

Well, that was a point. Although she'd seen a few of her work friends posting those quizzes on their socials. Maybe—hopefully—they fudged the data. "Still. You can do social engineering, spying, that sort of thing. Any info you gather is going to help your team."

"That's . . . not a terrible idea. I like the idea of covert data gathering. But the teams can't know that's what we're doing. We have to frame it as just capture the flag for the programmers. I'll get management and support together separately and fill them in—and they'll have a dedicated contact to share the information with. Our people ought to know better than to fall for social engineering anyway, so if they don't, that's on them."

Jess grinned. "Sneaky. I love it. Okay, so when do we start, how long does the game run, and what's the prize?"

"We should ask Tyler if the whole event has to take place this month or if we could kick it off but let it run longer."

That was a good point. It would be fun to let it run until a team won—because eventually someone would. They'd have to, wouldn't they? On the other hand, it might not take all that long.

Jess could already think of three people she wouldn't want on her team, because they'd be sure to flub something up right off the bat. "Okay. We can hash out the rest of the details tonight though, so we have a plan to present on Monday."

He smiled at her, and her muscles turned to jelly. "Maybe that's not all we could do tonight?"

Her thoughts zinged straight to that kiss—not that it took much to get her to go there. Her cheeks heated.

Ryan grinned. "I was going to suggest a movie, but I like the way you think."

Jess set down the weights and wiped sweat off her face with her towel. "A movie is a better idea. Maybe some dinner, too."

Ryan hit the Stop button on his treadmill and stepped off. He closed the distance between them and slid his arms around her.

Her belly quivered. She tipped her face up so she could meet his gaze. Was this really happening?

He brushed his lips across hers gently, pausing to linger a moment before easing back.

Jess sighed and laid her head on his shoulder. "Maybe we can work a few of those in, too?"

"More than likely." He kissed the top of her head. "I should tell your brother about this."

"No." Jess pulled away, shaking her head. "No, you absolutely should not."

"Jess. He's my best friend."

"And you know he'd be furious. At both of us." She hated the wheedle that edged into her voice, but she couldn't stop it. "Not yet. Just hold off a bit? Let us enjoy things the way they are for a little while before Christopher tries to convince us we need to stop."

"I don't think he would. Not when he sees how right this is."

"I love that you can say that, and mean it. But I know my

brother better than you do. In this case, I really think I do. Telling him is a bad plan, Ry. Just wait a little. For me?"

He searched her face before sighing and giving a short nod. "All right. If that's what you think is better."

"I really do." If Jess could figure out a way to never tell her brother what was going on between her and Ryan, she would. At some point, the truth would have to come out. Christopher and Ryan were best friends. Christopher was her big brother, and she loved him. She'd want him at their wedding. Her lips twitched. Maybe they could keep it quiet and just spring it on him right before the pastor came in.

No. That wouldn't work.

Ryan was right. They'd have to tell Christopher eventually.

Jess was content to let that day be far, far in the future.

6

J ess glanced at her brother as they found a place to wait in the crowded church foyer. She tried to keep her face from showing the concern she felt for him. Something was up between him and Stephanie. That much was obvious. Christopher wasn't talking, though, and neither was Ryan.

That last one left her a little peeved.

She was his girlfriend—and okay, that thrill would probably never go away—at least she hoped it wouldn't—but didn't that also mean he was supposed to tell her everything? They were partners, weren't they?

Except . . . loyalty to a best friend was admirable. She wouldn't say that was wrong. Ugh. Now she understood the complications of loving her brother's best friend a little better.

"Did you hear me?" Christopher nudged her with his elbow, frowning. "Where'd you go?"

"Sorry." Jess bit back the explanation. She still stood by not wanting to explain about her and Ryan dating. Especially if he was having trouble with his own girlfriend. "You're sure Stephanie won't be joining us? It's Valentine's Day."

"I'm sure." Christopher's voice was brusque. "Just drop it, okay?"

Jess held up her hands. "Sorry. Where's Ry?"

"I don't know. We can go in and get a seat if you're worried about missing the service." Christopher started toward the sanctuary doors.

"Don't you want to sit in the balcony?" He always pushed for the balcony.

"No."

"Because . . .?"

"Stop, would you? Look, there's Ryan." Christopher took off through the crowded foyer.

She hadn't been worried about finding a seat. She was just worried about her brother. She watched as Christopher greeted Ryan and the two men turned to look her way. Seeing Ryan, everything in Jess settled. She met his eyes and smiled.

He winked.

Christopher frowned and jerked his head toward the sanctuary doors. Fighting a sigh, Jess headed that direction. The past couple of weeks had been nice, with Chris meeting Stephanie to attend church together. Jess and Ryan had been able to sit by themselves, under the guise of giving her brother space. Now, Chris was back to sitting with them, and that put a damper on any Valentine's Day plans Jess might have been considering.

"Here, I saved you the aisle seat." Chris scooted down to make room for Jess.

She looked across her brother at Ryan.

He shrugged.

She tried to smile. "Thanks."

"What?"

"Nothing."

Chris frowned at her. "You're acting weird."

"No, I'm not." Jess plopped onto the pew and set her purse

on the floor under the seat in front of them. "Are we doing lunch after the service?"

"I guess. Not the deli." Chris looked at Ryan. "You in?"

"Sure. I don't have any other plans. Think we can actually get a table somewhere?"

"Oh." Christopher's scowl deepened.

"What if we got takeout and brought it back to my place. Or yours. Either one." Jess shrugged. "I bet we could get Thai pretty easily."

"Thai works for me." Ryan nudged Christopher. "What about you?"

"I guess." He looked like he was going to say more, but the choir filed in and the orchestra started up and he closed his mouth.

Jess stood with everyone else, ready to sing and worship. If her gaze kept straying to Ryan, well, he was looking her way, too. What a way to spend their first Valentine's Day.

Pastor Brown preached from First Corinthians, chapter thirteen. Jess had rolled her eyes when she heard the reference, but as usual, the pastor surprised her with something relevant. And challenging. Did she love in the way Christ asked her to? It was easier to love certain people some of the time, and that wasn't what God was after at all. Take Stephanie. Jess let her gaze dart to her brother.

She needed to find out what happened between him and Stephanie. Did he love her? It seemed so unlikely. The woman was . . . just not what Jess had imagined for him. But her opinion wasn't what counted. Just like Christopher's opinion of her and Ryan as a couple wasn't important. Except of course that she couldn't even think that without every muscle in her body tensing.

Her brother would not approve.

Why did she care so much, though?

Ryan was her person. She was sure of it.

So, what was she going to do?

For now? She'd kick that decision down the road a little bit.

At the end of the service, they split in different directions as they headed for their cars. Jess had bailed on the idea of carpooling, on the off chance she and Ryan had been able to figure out a way to get away and do something together. So much for that.

Ryan reached out to grab and squeeze her hand quickly. "Happy Valentine's Day."

She smiled and stepped closer after checking to see if her brother was out of sight. "You, too. This isn't what I was hoping for."

"Me, either, but your brother could use the people who love him right now."

She nodded. "Figured. Do you know what's going on?"

Ryan waggled his hand from side to side. "Kind of. I don't think I can share, though. He told me over chips and salsa."

"Sacred secret food. Got it." Jess sighed. "I guess I'll have to dig it out of him myself. But maybe not today. He seems so down."

"I tried to get him to do something for her for Valentine's Day. He was pretty adamant that it was the wrong move." Ryan lifted a shoulder. "You know how he gets when he's dug in. I let it go."

"Maybe that's what I ought to do." She bit her lip. "I hate that. He was finally starting to be happy. And while I can't say she's who I would have chosen for him? She was who he chose."

Ryan leaned close and pressed his lips to her hair. "You're who I choose."

Jess swallowed as her insides melted. "I really wish we didn't have to spend Valentine's Day with my brother."

"I know. But we'd better get going. If he beats us home with the food, he's going to start asking questions you don't want me to answer."

"It's not that I don't want you to answer—you know I'm not embarrassed of you, of this, don't you?"

"I guess. It's hard keeping secrets from my best friend."

She got that. Sort of. "Don't you think he has enough on his plate right now?"

"That's the only reason I'm agreeing." Ryan brushed his lips across her forehead. "Go on. I'll see you in a few."

She tried to smile but it felt flat. Was she doing this wrong? She wasn't trying to hurt Ryan. She just wanted to have him completely to herself for a while. Once Christopher found out—or anyone else—it was going to be drama.

She wasn't in the mood for drama.

Jess hurried to her car. Ryan was right about one thing, for sure: they both needed to get home before her brother did, or anything she wanted when it came to keeping things quiet about her relationship with Ryan was going to be moot.

"Does everyone understand how the hackathon is going to work?" Ryan glanced around the employees gathered. Most nodded. A few whispered to one another. But the overall feeling was one of excitement and anticipation. "Tomorrow will be server setup day. You'll have to get with your teams and divvy up the workload—well, you know what to do and how to do it. We only have a week, so next Friday at this time, the contest will be over. If there's a tie—meaning neither team is able to infiltrate the other's server and capture the sensitive information—then we'll have to figure out about the prize. I have ideas, but nothing firm."

Jess sent him a quizzical look.

Ryan shook his head slightly. Hopefully, she wouldn't ask right now, but he'd talked to Joe, briefly, about simply allowing the whole division to participate in the prize. There was no reason the corporate jet couldn't take everyone down to Florida for the weekend. It meant more trips, but even ferrying the winning team would have to be spread out over two or three weekends. Joe said that, in theory, that would work just as well. It was a matter of coordinating dates.

Ryan was reasonably sure there'd be a winner, even though he and Jess had excused themselves from participating.

Boy, had that gone over badly with Jess, but it wouldn't have been fair. At all.

He cleared his throat. "Okay. Get going. And remember, we're still expecting you to keep on top of your regular workload. That's part of the exercise."

"And the fun."

Ryan looked around. He didn't recognize who'd spoken, but the words brought some laughs and cheering. What a strange group they were. Maybe that was part of knowing your team, though—knowing that adding extra work could sometimes be a benefit rather than a drag.

"Good luck, everyone." Jess grinned. "And no, I won't help you. Ryan says it wouldn't be fair."

More chuckles as the crowd dispersed.

"He's not wrong."

Ryan stiffened and turned. "Special Agent Mosby. What brings you here?"

"We had a few more questions. Perhaps you'd care to join us in your office." The FBI man didn't bother to disguise his request as a question. "Ms. Ward, you might as well come along."

Jess nodded and pulled her phone from the pocket of her jeans. She started texting as she walked.

Was she getting in touch with her attorney? Hopefully.

They'd had a brief consult with the woman not long after Mosby's first visit, and as much as Ryan had hoped it would all be for nothing, Jess and her lawyer had been positive that Mosby would keep turning up.

Of course, he'd chosen the day that Jess made a joke about being a good hacker.

Mosby stood inside Ryan's office, behind his desk.

Ryan arched a brow. "I believe you're in my spot."

Mosby offered a dry chuckle, but he moved. "For now. I was wondering if either of you wanted to change your previous statement about the hacker known as Shadow-Warrior."

"Not me." Ryan took his seat and cocked his head to the side as he looked at Jess. "You?"

"Nope. Although I'd be happy to reach out to some of my friends—assuming you're willing to offer them some sort of immunity—and see if they have information." Jess shrugged. "It's all I can think of that might help."

"Ms. Ward, you can continue to try and hide behind this innocent act, but I know the truth, and I'm going to make it my life's work to see that you're locked up, where you belong, with no access to electronics for the rest of your days." Mosby's chest puffed out. "You don't fool me."

"Special Agent Mosby—that's your name, right?" Jess waited.

"You know it is."

She nodded. "I just needed to make sure you identified yourself for my attorney."

"For your . . . I don't understand." Mosby frowned. "You didn't invoke your right to counsel."

"Oh, well you didn't read me my rights, either, so we're probably both on the wrong side of the law here in that respect."

"If I might interject." The voice coming from Jess's phone held the twang of the deep South. "I don't know if you remember me, Special Agent Mosby, but we did meet at the first trial. I'm Amanda McDow."

"Ms. McDow." Mosby's face was a deep red.

Ryan fought the urge to smile.

"Oh, well, good. You remember. What's funny to me, is I believe I just heard you threaten my client, and I have to think your superiors might be interested to know about that along with your personal vendetta against Ms. Ward."

Mosby sputtered before collecting himself enough to be coherent. "I'm here on official business investigating several electronic incursions performed by someone using the handle ShadowWarrior. It's not unreasonable or a violation of my duty to speak with persons who have knowledge of the underbelly of the Internet where these sorts of behaviors occur."

"I'm sorry." Amanda spoke up, cutting him off. "I'm unclear when my client has been shown to have knowledge of the, what did you call it? The underbelly of the Internet? That's very poetic. However, Ms. Ward is a computer security specialist. Not some sort of hacking miscreant. It's true that she's called on to test the security of systems of her paying clients and those who have awarded business to the cyber division of Robinson Enterprises, but I don't see where or how that would overlap with the object of your investigation. Furthermore, I'm informed by Ms. Ward that after you last visited her at her place of employment, she and Mr. Foster located a listening device in his office. I've made a few phone calls and have yet to discover the wiretap warrant that would have authorized this placement."

"Would you like some water, Agent Mosby? You're looking peaky." Ryan started to stand. The man definitely looked unwell. "Perhaps you ought to sit?"

Mosby jabbed his index finger in the direction of Jess. "I'm watching you, Ward. Be afraid."

The Special Agent spun and stormed from the office.

"Mr. Foster? Perhaps you ought to call down to security for your building to ensure Special Agent Mosby reaches the exit safely." Amanda's voice held the faintest hint of a smile. "Jess? You really need to be proactive here. Say the word, and I'll get things rolling. The man is harassing you. He clearly has a vendetta. I'm not convinced you're safe."

Jess sighed. "Yeah, fine. I just don't want to be on their radar."

"You're already there, hon. Sitting back and hiding isn't going to make it go away. And if you do know this ShadowWarrior character? Maybe you ought to let them know it's time to keep a low profile for a few months."

"I'll pass it along to people who might be able to pass it along the rest of the way."

"Good girl."

Ryan hung up his desk phone. "Security confirms that Mosby just stormed out of the building. They also apologized for letting him up, but they have instructions to cooperate with the authorities. They were a little surprised when he showed up without his partner."

"That is curious, isn't it? I have a few strings I can pull to see if I can find out more information. Leave this to me, but keep me on speed dial. I'm sorry, Jess. I really thought this was over when the trial ended."

"Yeah, me too. Thanks, Amanda. Keep me posted." Jess tapped End on her cell and sank into Ryan's guest chair.

"Hey." He came around and dragged the other chair close, sitting so his knees bumped hers. "This is going to go away. You're going to be okay."

She shook her head. Her eyes glistened with unshed tears. "Is it? Am I? Maybe I should just—"

Ryan put a finger to her lips and shook his head slightly. He wouldn't put it past Mosby to try to plant another listening device. "What you ought to do is head back to your desk. I know you have work that needs to be done. And so do I. We're not going to solve the mystery of Mosby right this red-hot second."

"I don't like that you're right." She leaned forward and rested her forehead on his. "I'm going to have to tell Christopher."

Ryan winced. "Yeah. I wish I could say you didn't, but with the lawyer involved again, it's better that he find out from you before things get any worse."

"Maybe I'll head down to his office and talk to him now." Jess scooted back so she could stand. "Thanks, Ry."

"For what?" He hadn't done anything—and that burned in his gut. He'd wanted to slug Mosby, but that wouldn't have accomplished anything beyond hurting his hand and getting him in trouble. Probably arrested. That definitely wasn't going to help Jess.

"For being here. For caring."

He stood and, after a quick glance out his open door into the hallway to check that it was empty, pulled her close. "I love you."

"I love you, too." She leaned up and pressed her lips to his.

He sank in, deepening the kiss despite the warning bell ringing in his head. They were at work, with his office door open. Anyone could see. He pulled back. "Go talk to your brother. Then why don't you go home? It's a few hours early, but I know you've put in extra this week."

"I—" Jess nodded. "Yeah, okay. Am I going to see you tonight?"

"Wouldn't miss it for the world. Dinner after the workout? I could grab some Indian." His stomach rumbled. That sounded amazing—how long was it before dinner?

"Perfect. Just like you." Jess squeezed his hand and slipped out of his office.

Ryan watched her go before sighing and pinching the bridge of his nose. Jess hadn't used the ShadowWarrior accounts since sending that large batch of information to her contact. Why was

Mosby still chasing it down? And why wouldn't he believe the false trail she'd laid? He'd looked it over—it was convincing. It really did look like ShadowWarrior was a disaffected member of the trafficking ring. At least to him. And to Jess.

So why not to Mosby?

Jess had wanted to poke around for information about the Special Agent. Maybe Ryan should encourage her to go ahead.

Or maybe that would just cause more problems.

He sank into his desk chair and stared at his monitor. Keeping secrets was his least favorite thing and right now it seemed like his whole life revolved around two of them: the secret activities of the woman he loved, and the fact that he loved her in the first place.

He closed his eyes and tried to pray for clarity. He wasn't going to be able to unravel this situation without some divine guidance.

So why did it feel like God was so very far away?

7

Ryan closed the door to the condo and dropped his bag in the corner. "Christopher? You home, man?"

"In the kitchen."

Ryan toed off his shoes and headed that direction. "You staying in tonight?"

"Yeah." Christopher leaned against the island. "I put a frozen pizza in the oven. If you're interested, I'm sure there'll be plenty."

"I'm going to work out and then maybe swing up to Jess's place so we can check in on the hackathon. There ought to be a little monitoring we can do by now. At least see if both teams have their servers set up and secured." Ryan shrugged, hoping it appeared nonchalant. "Unless you need me here?"

"Nah, that's fine. I think it's hilarious that the two of you found a way to make people do more work and they're actually excited about it. If we'd tried that in government services, we would've had a riot." Christopher shook his head.

Ryan grinned. "How'd the big glam party at Joe's go last night?"

"It was good. Honestly, the food was some of the best I've ever had. If Stephanie and I were still together, I'd take her on a date to that place. It's in Arlington—Season's Bounty I think it's called."

"Yeah? I'll keep it in mind."

"Uh-huh. You're less likely to go on a date than I am. When's the last time you did anything romantic with a woman?" Christopher rolled his eyes. "At least I'm out there trying."

Ryan bit his tongue. Would Jess like to go out, instead? He'd dropped the Indian takeout at her place on his way home, but it would keep. She could eat it for lunch tomorrow and Saturday, if she wanted. Maybe he'd suggest going out as an option. It'd mean he'd need to sneak a change of clothes into his bag when he went down to exercise, but that was doable. Especially since he'd already said he was going up to Jess's place. "Stephanie hasn't thawed any?"

Christopher shook his head. "It's fine. She's the epitome of professional and, at the end of the day, she deserves the position. I think I'm going to bow out. There are other jobs—although I'd be fine to keep working for her if she'd be all right with it. I talked to Joe a little last night. We're going to arrange a time to talk more."

Ryan frowned. "I don't want you to leave. I like knowing you're around the Robinson Enterprises building if I need you."

"Whatever. We hardly ever see each other during the day. It wouldn't matter if I worked somewhere else in Tyson's. It's not like I'm moving out of the area and you'd have to find a new roommate." Christopher's smile didn't quite reach his eyes. "Speaking of seeing people during the workday. Jess swung by to talk to me about the FBI."

Ryan nodded. "Good."

"Why didn't you tell me the first time they came?"

"Because she asked me not to."

Christopher frowned, but nodded slowly. "All right. I can give you that. How worried do you think I need to be?"

Ryan held his thumb and forefinger about two inches apart. "This much? The McDow woman sounds like she's on it—in fact, she seemed like she was going to take great pleasure in doing something proactive to get him shut down. It feels like she's the right person to have in Jess's corner."

"Okay. If that changes, I want you to promise to tell me. Even if Jess says not to. She's too independent for her own good. I can't help her if I don't know I need to."

Ryan's instinct was to agree, but Jess would never go for that. If she asked him not to tell, he needed to respect that. Jess needed to be able to trust him. "I don't want to break her trust."

"Come on, man. You're my best friend, and you have an in with this situation that I don't. How would you like it if the tables were turned?" The oven timer beeped and Christopher moved to take his pizza from the oven. He slid it onto the island and dug through drawers to find the pizza cutter.

"I get that. But at the same time, I'm her friend, too." So much more than friends, but it was enough of a baseline to work from. It had to be. "We work together. We're in this contest together. I can't just go behind her back if she asks me not to. But I promise I'll try to convince her to keep you in the loop. It's the best I can offer."

Christopher scowled. "I guess it'll have to do. Maybe I need to have a chat with my sister about stealing my best friend."

Ryan forced a laugh. "Oh, please. Do I need to stay here tonight and prove my loyalty? Cause I will."

"No. It's fine. Go work out—you're a regular health nut these days."

"Yeah. I'm finding I kind of enjoy it. And I owe it all to you."

"Remember that, will you? You owe me." Christopher's grin was more relaxed this time. "I guess I'm glad you'll be hanging with Jess tonight, too. Maybe you can keep her from doing something stupid like trying to dig up information on this Mosby character."

"Believe me, the thought occurred. I'm glad we have the hackathon to monitor. Or maybe I ought to see if she wants to try that restaurant you mentioned and get her out of her condo completely."

"You can try. It's kind of a date place, but it's not like you and Jess haven't eaten together before. Getting her away from temptation might be the better choice." Christopher shrugged. "Either way. Thanks for looking out for my baby sister. It's good to know I can trust you with her."

Ryan swallowed. Trusting him with her probably didn't include long, deep kisses that stirred both their appetites for more than food. His stomach twisted. He hated being stuck in the middle like this. But what else was he supposed to do? "You know I love her, too."

Christopher snorted. "Yeah, I guess we can share the little twerp. Thanks. And hey, more pizza for me."

"Right. Enjoy yourself. I think I'm going to change and head down. If we try the restaurant, I'll let you know what I think."

"That's a deal. Tell Jess hi."

Ryan nodded and headed toward his room to put on sweats. Was this going to get easier? Ever?

The truth will set you free.

He closed his eyes as the verse floated through his head. That was one he'd learned early at his mother's insistence. Somehow, he had to get Jess on board with spilling the beans. Maybe, if they could figure out a way to fix things between Christopher and Stephanie, his friend would be more open to his sister finding love, too.

It was something to think about. *God? I could really use some direction here.*

JESS SLID into the back pew of the sanctuary. The Wednesday evening prayer meeting had already started, but no one did more than turn briefly to look and smile before resuming singing. Where was . . . there. Up at the front, Stephanie stood with everyone else, but it was as if there was a circle of padding around her separating her from the group. She was obviously alone. Completely, one hundred percent, alone.

Jess frowned, her heart aching for both Stephanie and her brother. Was there any way to fix things? Or even try? She didn't know what had happened. Gentle prodding of Christopher wasn't getting her anywhere, and Ryan was convinced that he needed to protect the secret chips-and-salsa-bond. And okay, fine, Jess could appreciate that. She'd asked him to keep secrets, too. Was counting on it, for that matter. She couldn't—or at least she shouldn't—be mad when he gave the same courtesy to other people he loved.

He loved her.

It made her smile.

Even with all the madness of the contest at work and the situation with the FBI, she finally had a man who knew her and loved her anyway.

God was like that.

Jess sat when the singing ended and opened her Bible app when Pastor Brown started to speak, but her mind wasn't engaging. Why had she never made the connection before? God knew her better than anyone—better than she knew herself—and He loved her. Unconditionally. Even when she was unlovable.

Wasn't that exactly what everyone craved?

So how could she help Christopher see that it was probably something Stephanie wanted, too. Her brother was in love—that much was obvious to Jess. Maybe because she knew him so well, or maybe because it was obvious to someone who was also in love. Either way, he needed to figure out how to fix things.

Jess was going to do whatever she could to help.

Why did it matter?

Was it because she was looking for ways to lessen the odds of him blowing up when she told him about Ry? Probably. She didn't want to lose either of them—she needed her brother and his best friend in her life. But their relationships were changing. Both of them. And there was a part of her that mourned the simpler times, even when the new relationship was what she yearned for more than anything else.

Pastor Brown ended his mini-lesson, and the people in the sanctuary began to shift, forming little circles with the others nearby. She smiled when the older woman in front of her turned and beckoned her closer.

"Come join our prayer circle, dear."

Jess scooted closer.

"Do you have the prayer list?" The woman held up a single sheet of paper.

"No. Was I supposed to pick that up somewhere?"

"They hand them out before we start. It's okay, you can share mine. Do you have anything you want to add on?"

Jess considered for a moment. "You know what, I do. My brother and his girlfriend are having some trouble. I really believe that God brought them together, but I'm not sure they're going to figure that out before it's too late."

The old woman patted Jess's hand. "It's never too late. What are their names?"

"Christopher and Stephanie." Jess pressed her lips together. Should she have come up with fake names? Well, too late now. At least, she was far enough in the back that it was unlikely she'd been overheard. Besides, it wasn't as if those were super unique names.

The woman jotted the information down and nodded to the three others who had merged into their circle. "Anyone else?"

No one spoke.

"Then let's pray. I'll start." The woman lowered her head.

Jess listened and prayed quietly in her head for wisdom and words. And for the situation with the FBI. She was still convinced that she had done the right thing gathering the intel that had cleared the way for those kids to be set free, but she *had* crossed lines. Amanda seemed confident that she could make it go away. But how long would it take?

When prayer meeting was over, Jess still wasn't sure what she should do. She'd come with a vague plan to get Stephanie's side of things. Now? That didn't seem so wise. Her brother was a big boy, fully capable of solving his own problems. Most of the time.

He didn't seem convinced there was anything to fight for with Stephanie, and that was frustrating.

She'd let it go. Jess wouldn't exactly appreciate Christopher meddling in her business, so she might as well do him the courtesy of staying out of his. With a nod to the group who had prayed together, she gathered her things and stood, then slipped out of the pew and started toward the door.

"Jess?"

She stopped and turned.

"You're Jess, right?" Stephanie frowned at her. "You work in Cyber?"

"That's me. And you're Stephanie and you work with my boneheaded brother."

Stephanie laughed, but it ended as a sigh. "Yeah. How is he?"

Jess cocked her head to the side. "Don't you still see him every day?"

"Yeah, I guess. But I figure he puts on a happy face. That's what I do." Stephanie shrugged. "It's natural, right?"

"It is." Jess considered a moment before adding, "You want to grab some coffee?"

"I don't . . . why?"

Jess grinned. "We can trash talk Chris if you want. Mostly, I'd like to get to know the woman my brother's in love with."

"He's wasting his time. I was serious when I said we were over. If he sent you here—"

"Whoa." Jess held up a hand. "No one sent me anywhere. I came to prayer meeting because Chris said it wasn't what I thought it would be. He was right. I'll admit to having considered sitting beside you, but you'll notice I didn't. And you approached me, not the other way around. So you can chill. I'll rescind the coffee offer and be on my way. Have a good night."

"Wait."

Jess stopped. Thought for a second. Crossed her arms and turned, eyebrows lifted.

Stephanie sighed. "It's not easy for me. I like your brother. A lot. But I can't be someone who I'm not."

"No one's asking you to."

Stephanie's head bounced side to side. "Kinda feels that way."

"People change. They grow."

"They do. I'm working on it. But I also need to know that someone I'm with—the person I love? They need to love me for who I am, not who I might someday end up being. That's just pressure that neither one of us needs in our life."

Okay, that made sense. "If Chris made you think he wouldn't love you until you met some arbitrary goal, then he's an idiot. I'm sorry for him. And I'm sorry for you. That's not who I would ever have said my brother was."

"It's okay. It's not like he's the first person in my life to be that way. He probably won't be the last. I know who I am—good and bad."

"But do you know who he is?"

"I think I do, yeah." Stephanie shrugged. "If you're still interested in that coffee, I can always use caffeine."

"What about a friend?" Jess wasn't positive, but it sure seemed like a friend was a more important need for this woman than coffee.

"That too." Stephanie smiled. "There's a decent place across the street."

"I know it. I'll meet you over there." Jess turned and headed toward her car. Her brother was an idiot of the first order if he wasn't going to fight for this woman. Oh, sure, she had some sharp edges, but really, who didn't? Some people were just better at hiding them.

8

Jess watched her brother storm out of his condo, then looked at Ryan. "Should I not have pushed that hard?"

Ryan reached for her hand and squeezed it. "No. It's what he needed. He's been moping around long enough. At some point, the two of them need to figure it out—or at least clear the air—and if you saw her crying in the stairwell? Then he needed to know that."

"Yeah. That's true." Jess paused. "I liked her. We had coffee Wednesday after prayer meeting and I think, underneath it all, she's got a tender heart that's been bruised too many times, so she hides it."

"I mean, I get that, but she still needs to figure it out."

Jess frowned. "What do you mean?"

"I mean she's kind of a hard butt. You hear things—a lot of her employees aren't her biggest fans."

"Because she's blunt and no nonsense? Like a man would be?" Jess lifted her eyebrows. "Or have I missed when you're all sweet and stroky when someone is behind on a deadline?"

Ryan blew out a breath. "Okay. You're probably right. If I concede that there's a double standard in the workplace that allows men to behave in a way that would be deemed unacceptable for women, can we not spend the next ten minutes fighting about it?"

"You think we'd be finished fighting in ten minutes?"

"I think I have ten minutes—on the outside—before the first of the guys shows up for Bible study. I also think I would rather spend those ten minutes kissing you than arguing about workplace dynamics."

Jess grinned. "All right. I accept your concession."

"I hoped you would." Ryan stood and tugged her to her feet before cradling her close and lowering his mouth to hers.

Jess sighed and disappeared into the kiss. What was it that made such a simple thing—the meeting of mouths—so magical? Ryan's hands skimmed across her shoulders and down her back, leaving a trail of fire in their wake. A tiny part of her brain registered the danger of the situation. It would be so easy to let herself get caught up. To let things continue along the natural progression of where these sensations were leading.

She broke away and stepped back, pressing her lips together. "I should go."

"I don't want you to." His eyes reflected the things she felt burning through her body. "But you're right. You probably should."

"I love you." Jess leaned forward and kissed him quickly.

"We have to tell your brother. Soon, Jess." Ryan swallowed. "Please?"

"I know." She could know something and still dread it, couldn't she? "Let's see if he can work things out with Stephanie. Maybe that'll put him in a better frame of mind."

"I don't like sneaking around. Or lying to my best friend."

"Lying?" She shoved her hands in her pockets. "You shouldn't have to lie."

"I didn't know what else to do when he got all bristly big

brother and asked point-blank what was going on with you and me."

The blood drained out of her head and she dropped back into her seat. Her voice came out as a mix between a whisper and a croak. "When?"

"Just now. When you were getting his keys."

Jess covered her face. This was bad. "I'm sorry."

"Me, too. I won't do it again. I love you. I'm not ashamed of that." Ryan gently pried her hands away from her face. "Are you?"

"No. Of course I'm not. It's just that he's so . . ."

Ryan's lips twitched. "He definitely is. But that doesn't change anything. I don't want to lose my best friend. I absolutely don't—but when I say that now, I mean you."

Her eyes filled. "I feel the same way."

"So we'll tell him. And he can get on board, or I'll find someplace else to live for a little bit. Until I can live with you."

She blinked. Live with . . . he wanted to get married? Something clutched at her heart and Jess wasn't positive what it was. Some was definitely excitement and love. But . . . marriage? That was so serious. So adult.

So fast.

He was watching her.

She stretched her lips into a smile and stood, stepping into him and wrapping her arms around his waist. She pressed her face into his shoulder and breathed in the scent of fabric softener and that unique combination that flooded her senses with the knowledge that this was Ryan. It couldn't be anyone else.

And it was home.

His arms came around her loosely. "This week? We'll tell him this week. Okay?"

Jess nodded. There was no other possible response. She

could hear the resolve in his voice. If she didn't get on board, Ryan would do it anyway. "This week. Maybe on Thursday."

"Why Thursday?"

"Because we leave Friday on the trip to Florida with the first wave of the blue team?"

"Right. Hackathon winners." Ryan grinned. "Smart. And I'm still surprised the red team didn't manage to fend them off."

Jess chuckled. "It was social engineering at its finest. Also, apparently, Marley and Ned are now dating. Provided Ned's friends don't get on his case too badly about having been so distracted by her flirting that he forgot to shore up the vulnerabilities on the server."

"Details. I can attest that women are distracting." He started to lean toward her and jolted when someone pounded on the front door. "Oh, man. There's the guys."

"I'll get going. I love you. It's going to be okay."

"I think that's my line."

Jess didn't care who said it, but someone needed to keep it going on repeat in her head or she was going to be a basket case.

She loved Ryan. Wanted him in her life. But telling Christopher?

That was going to be a nightmare.

RYAN PACED the length of his bedroom. All week, he'd been practicing what he'd say to Christopher. And all week, the knot in his stomach had gotten tighter. He had tried to act unconcerned when Jess brought it up, but he understood what she was saying.

Still. He didn't want to lie. And he didn't want to hide the best thing that had ever happened in his life. Being with Jess—being able to hold her and kiss her? He didn't want to let go of that.

Would Christopher really expect him to?

Surely not. Not now, when his friend had patched things up with Stephanie and understood what it was to be in a relationship with the right person. Finally.

And okay, maybe it made him stupid that it took so long to realize the woman he loved was right there under his nose this whole time, but he'd take it if it meant he got to keep Jess.

His phone buzzed. He tapped the screen, his lips curving when he saw Jess's name. He opened her text and took a deep breath that he let out slowly. Okay. Showtime.

Ryan padded down the hall to the front door.

"You going out?" Christopher looked up from his laptop.

"Nah. Your sister's here." Ryan continued on his way, but he didn't miss the quizzical look his friend shot him. Because of course he didn't understand why she wouldn't knock or use her key. Or, barring any of that, why she'd tell Ryan and not him.

This was the problem with having been friends for so long. Ryan could probably script the upcoming conversation . . . and none of it was going to be good. He fully understood why Jess hadn't wanted to say something, but it seemed like it was going to be better for everyone involved if they were honest and laid all the cards on the table now. If Christopher found out from someone else?

Ryan shook his head. Hoo boy. No. He didn't want to even imagine how that would work out.

He opened the door. Seeing Jess, everything in him relaxed. She brought a sense of peace with her everywhere she went. He checked over his shoulder before darting in to kiss her hello. "Hi."

"Hi." She bit her lip. "You're sure this is the right thing to do?"

He nodded. It was the right thing. The smart thing? Probably not. The smart thing would have been never to open the door to a relationship with Jess in the first place. He'd been doing so well at that until this contest.

"Okay. I trust you." She slipped her hand into his and clung to it.

Ryan closed the door.

Jess started toward the living room, still holding on to Ryan's hand.

Oh. They were just going in guns blazing. That wasn't quite how Ryan had pictured starting things off, but people said that ripping the bandage off fast hurt less. He pushed away the sense of dread that threatened to drown him.

"Chris? You got a second?" Jess still clung to Ryan's hand as she stood by their coffee table.

"What's up?" Christopher looked over from his computer. His eyes darted down to their hands. Then back up to Jess. Then over to Ryan. His features settled in a stony glare. "What's going on?"

Jess inched closer to Ryan.

He squeezed her hand. "Um. Jess and I wanted to tell you something."

"No." Christopher shook his head. "Not an option. Not happening. No way. No how. And frankly? I expected better of both of you."

"You haven't even heard what we have to say." Anger began to simmer in Ryan's chest. He'd known Chris wasn't going to jump up and down for joy, but the guy was usually reasonable.

Christopher pointed at their joined hands. "Does it have to do with that?"

"Yes, but—"

"Are you pregnant? Did he take advantage of you?" Chris surged to his feet, his laptop toppling to the sofa. "I ought to—"

"What? No. Stop being a jerk." Jess dropped Ryan's hand and

crossed her arms. "You really think that of me? Of your best friend?"

"I don't know! I never expected this of either of you. Maybe I don't know you as well as I thought I did." Chris's voice edged up in volume.

"Funny." Now Jess was practically yelling, too. "Because I knew this was exactly what was going to happen and it's why I made Ryan promise not to tell!"

"How long have you been lying to me?" Now Chris whirled on Ryan.

Ryan shook his head. "I only lied once and that was Monday."

Christopher breathed heavily through his nose, his chest heaving. "And how long has this been going on?"

Ryan glanced at Jess, who was glaring at her brother. She was clearly not going to be any help. He worked to keep his voice calm. "About a month."

"Seriously? Wow. So much for being my best friend."

"What was I supposed to do? Ask permission?"

Chris's jaw tightened.

"Exactly. If I'd come to you and said, 'Hey bro, turns out I've fallen in love with your sister and would like to pursue a relationship with her, would that be okay?' what would you have said?" Ryan tucked his hands into his pockets. It was that or give in to the urge to punch his friend. That wouldn't help things. Even if it might help Ryan feel better.

"I don't know, because it's not what happened."

"Oh, please." Jess pushed her brother's shoulder. Chris lost his balance and landed on the couch. "You would have gone off on a rant about your baby sister and how she was off-limits to every man ever made. I know this, because the few times I've dated and gone ahead and let you meet the guy, you've explained to them how I'm too young to be involved with someone. Then you come to me and explain why the guy was wrong for me. Well, let's hear it. Because this time, the guy is your oldest, best friend. Explain to me how he's unworthy of me."

"I'd be curious to hear that justification, too." Ryan slid closer to Jess and hooked his arm around her waist. "Am I good enough to be your friend but not good enough for your sister?"

"It's different." Chris clenched his hands in his lap. "You have to understand that."

"No. I really don't." Ryan scowled at Chris. "I can't count how many times you've talked to me about wishing your sister would find a Godly man. Someone who would love her the way Christ loves the Church. Someone who could cherish her and see all the beautiful things about her that she hides from the general public. Well, that's me. I see that. I know that. Because I've known her forever. I've probably loved her for half that time, but been too scared to admit it to myself. And if you tell me I have to choose between her and my best friend, I'll tell you you're wrong. Because they're the same person now—and when I choose the person who knows me best, who loves me most, I'm choosing Jess. We didn't tell you because we were looking for permission. We told you because we respect you enough to know you deserve the truth." Ryan kissed the top of Jess's head. "Come on, baby. Let's go get some dinner and give your brother a chance to figure out whether or not he's going to be an adult."

Ryan hurried to get shoes, keys, and his wallet. How long Christopher was going to stew was anyone's guess, but he didn't want to be around for it. He had to believe that, at some point, Chris would realize that Jess couldn't have done better. That Ryan couldn't have done better. This thing between them was right.

Christopher didn't look up from his computer when Ryan passed through the living room. Jess was hovering by the front door.

"You okay?" Ryan kept his voice low as he opened the door for her.

She shook her head. "I really didn't think it would be that bad."

He snorted.

"What?"

Ryan shrugged. "Just seems to me you didn't think about it then. You're his baby sister—he sees you like you were when you were six or seven. And I get it, I spent a lot of time trying to keep you relegated to that age, too. It was easier than admitting you'd blossomed into this incredible woman."

"So you're attracted to my brain?" Jess looked up at him, pouting slightly.

With a laugh, he kissed her before reaching for the elevator call button. "That's part of the attraction, for sure. But I'm never going to complain about how well you fill out your jeans and T-shirts."

Jess glanced down at the Pink Floyd T-shirt she'd thrown on at random before coming to get this over with. "You don't mind my fashion sense?"

He almost asked what fashion sense, but cut off the question before it worked its way out. "Nope. It's part of who you are."

The elevator arrived and they stepped in.

Jess hit the button for the parking garage. "What did you want to eat?"

"I don't know. What about you?"

"What if we went to Season's Bounty again?"

He nodded. He'd enjoyed that. The food was fresh and tasty. Maybe it was steeper in price than a chain or something fast, but that was offset by the quality. "Sounds like a plan."

Jess's smile didn't reach her eyes.

"Hey. Chin up. Your brother will come around."

"What if he doesn't?"

Ryan hit the button to unlock his car and opened the passenger door for Jess. He didn't know how to answer her. He'd meant every word he'd said to Christopher—and yet, he didn't want to lose his best male friend, either.

Christopher had to come around.

If he didn't?

Really and truly choosing between them was going to shatter Ryan's heart no matter what.

9

Ryan tossed his overnight bag into the storage above the seats of the private jet. It wasn't one of the super fancy jets with couches and conversation groupings of big recliners. Too bad. Still, the rows of seats were a lot like what he'd seen walking through first class on a normal flight, so it was definitely better than anything he'd ever afforded on his own dime.

Jess poked him in the side and grinned. "This is amazing."

"Nice to see how the other half lives, isn't it?" He smiled. "You want the window?"

"Sure. I don't fly a lot. It's always an adventure." Jess slipped past him and into her seat.

One third of the members of the winning hackathon team were filing onto the plane, chattering with one another as they took their seats and stowed their bags. The rest of the team would get the trip in the following two weekends. All things considered, it was great of Joe to agree to fly the winners down to his Florida house on the beach for a weekend. A little sun, sand, and surf were sure to be just what they all needed.

The losing team—and really, they hadn't lost by much—had

all been given the day off with pay, so no one should be too upset. Maybe they hadn't gotten to hit the beach, but at least they weren't slaving away in the office.

Joe and his fiancée, Cynthia, were the last on the plane. They settled in the seat just in front of Ryan and Jess, then Joe peeked through the space between the seats. "Thanks for letting us tag along."

Ryan laughed. "I think we're the ones who should be saying thank you. This is incredible."

"Well, I should go ahead and admit this isn't my jet. Mine only holds ten, max. But it's an easy enough thing to rent something to handle a larger crowd when it's needed." Joe grinned. "It's a perk of the job, for sure."

"One I'm grateful he's starting to have time to enjoy." Cynthia leaned over. "And I'm pleased it worked out for me to get some time off, too. I haven't actually seen our Florida house yet."

Ryan shook his head. He couldn't fathom the ability to rent a jet or buy a beach house whenever the whim struck. Joe worked hard—and had for years—so it wasn't as if he was some kind of billionaire playboy. But still. Would heading up Cyber eventually get Ryan to the place where he could be so casual about money?

Billionaire was a stretch. Realistically, Joe had only hit that number because of the multiple business income streams. But multi-millionaire was a distinct possibility.

Ryan glanced over at Jess. What would it be like for the two of them to jet off for the weekend? He'd love to take her to Paris. Or Rome. Or anywhere her heart desired to go.

She'd talked about traveling a lot when she was younger, but in the last several years, those conversations had tapered off. Was it because she didn't want to anymore? Or was there something else?

"You okay?" Ryan slipped his fingers through hers. "You're

not nervous about flying, are you?"

"No. Nothing like that. I've always wanted to travel." She squeezed his hand but then tugged hers loose.

Ryan fought a frown. Why wouldn't she want to hold his hand? They were out in public now, weren't they? They'd told Christopher—and okay, fine, he wasn't excited about it, but he'd deal. Which meant they didn't have to hide their relationship at all. Didn't it?

Ryan arranged his hand on the arm rest, palm up. He'd leave it to her. For now.

"Ladies and gentlemen, this is the captain speaking. Please be sure you're seated and your seatbelts are fastened. We'll be taking off in just a few minutes. Flight time to Florida should be just about two hours. Enjoy your trip, and if you need anything, Melissa will be happy to serve you."

Ryan glanced over at Jess, who sat peering out the window. "Do you want something to drink? We probably have time to get something before we take off."

"I'm good."

"Okay. Let me know if I can get you something."

"I will."

Ryan shook his head. Something was up with her. Was it just Christopher? Or was Jess questioning more than her brother's reaction?

He swallowed but it did nothing to ease the lump in his throat.

Now that he had Jess in his life, he didn't want to lose her.

He leaned back in his seat and closed his eyes. He wasn't necessarily a nervous traveler, but it wasn't as if he did it often. Between that and the fact that he hadn't slept well after the blowup with Christopher the night before, maybe the best thing to do was nap and pray for things to be back to normal when they got to Florida.

Ryan drifted in and out of sleep for the duration of the flight. It wasn't restful. He was grateful when the captain finally came on the PA system to let them know they were beginning their descent.

Since it was a private plane, getting through the airport to the waiting cars was easier than when he'd traveled solo. Jess was still acting weird, though. She wouldn't hold his hand. She only answered his questions with one or two words. Finally, he stopped trying. Maybe she was as tired as he was. That had to be it, didn't it?

The ride to Joe's Florida house was full of laughter from the members of the victorious blue team. Even split between three vehicles, it was clear that everyone had come prepared to party. And that not everyone in Cyber had the same sense of decorum as Ryan had anticipated.

This could potentially turn out very poorly.

Joe's home was massive and sprawling. And right on the private neighborhood beach. Everyone got their room assignments and broke off to get settled and change into beach clothes. Joe had mentioned a barbeque by the water for dinner.

Ryan claimed a bed in one of the double occupancy guest rooms, barely noticing who else would be in there with him. It was just a place to sleep. His plan was to find Jess and hang with her. He thought that was her plan, too.

But maybe he was wrong.

His stomach knotted. After all this time, had he ruined things with Christopher only to turn around and find out that things weren't going to work between him and Jess, after all? He hadn't done anything but love her and want to be open about it.

Why wouldn't she talk to him?

After changing into shorts, he headed down the stairs, barely noticing the grandeur that surrounded him as he searched chattering groups for Jess. He finally gave up and headed out the back door to the beach.

There were people gathered here, too, but it was more spread out. It was a little chilly to swim, but a handful of brave souls were out in the waves nearly to their waist. No thanks.

Ryan wandered to where the large grills were set up and caterers were working. The smell of charcoal wafted on the ocean breeze. His stomach rumbled in response.

"You doing okay?" Joe fell into step beside Ryan.

"I guess. This is generous of you. Thanks again. I know the prize was a big motivator for our game."

"I thought your game was clever. It demonstrated how well you know your people. They wouldn't have been happy with something like a fancy cocktail party or a scavenger hunt."

"Someone did a scavenger hunt?"

Joe nodded. "The video game team. It started with candy bars taped to paper hearts, but that was the opening to the quest. I think quest is the actual word that was used."

Ryan laughed. Knowing the team was definitely a bonus. "A quest is right up their alley. Was there a boss battle at the end?"

"Come to think of it, yeah. They had to deal with my admin." Joe chuckled. "She can be fierce when she's guarding my time. Thankfully, she was in on it, so she could play along without actually being irritated."

"That's definitely a good thing." Joe's admin was scary. It was probably part of her job description—be scary and efficient—but Ryan still avoided her at all costs.

"How are you and Jess getting along?"

"What do you mean?" Was it obvious that they were having problems? That wouldn't be good.

"Just in general. Some of the teams have had a harder time finding their stride than others. Yours wasn't one I worried about, honestly, but on the plane it seemed like maybe that was a miscalculation on my part." Joe shrugged. "You don't have to talk to me about it, obviously. But sometimes it can help."

"I love her." Ryan shook his head and stared out at the water. Well, he was in for it now. He might as well tell the whole thing. "We've been friends forever, it feels like. I don't know if you knew that."

"Sure. Jessica Ward. Younger sister of Christopher Ward. Your roommate. I do try to keep on top of the basics."

"Roommate and best friend since elementary school." Ryan shoved his hands in his pockets. "Although that might be over now. Christopher was displeased that Jess and I are dating."

"You told him."

"It seemed like a good idea at the time. I didn't want him to find out accidentally, you know? That would've been a slap in the face. Although, based on his reaction, just dating his sister was the same thing. So . . . there was no winning. And now Jess is acting weird and I'm beginning to wonder if I've lost both of them."

"Hmm. And the FBI situation?"

Ryan turned to look at Joe, eyebrows raised.

"Come on now. I know I have a reputation as someone who keeps tabs on the goings on in each of the companies. You didn't think I'd have the details? Special Agent Mosby and his friend came to see me before they were ever given permission to seek you out. Not that I think they were looking for permission, but I gave it. I'm not going to stand by if someone I hired was breaking the law. Even someone whose work I admire and respect. But I also don't happen to believe Jess is doing anything that would warrant FBI involvement."

Ryan sorted through Joe's words. Did he know or just suspect that Jess hadn't completely hung up her hacking shoes? "The second time—when Mosby came on his own—Jess got her attorney involved."

"Good. I won't tolerate unfounded harassment of my people. I told them that when they came to me." Joe frowned and got his phone out of his pocket. "I think I'll get in touch with the company's lawyers and have them reach out to Jess'. Is that Amanda McDow still?"

Ryan nodded. Did the man know everything?

"Like I said, I try to be informed. I was cautioned about hiring her—Mosby has a bit of a one-track mind when it comes to Jessica—but I thought gainful employment might help keep her on the straight and narrow."

Ryan snorted. "That's almost word for word what Christopher said when he talked to me about trying to get her a spot. I don't know if we succeeded, but we definitely keep her busy."

"Human trafficking is a horrible thing. The government doesn't seem able to handle shutting it down on their own. I'm not going to say that laypeople shouldn't be involved." Joe smiled before glancing down at his phone and tapping on the screen.

He knew. Joe Robinson knew all about Jess and her after-hours activity? That didn't seem like a good thing. Even if he didn't know and just suspected, it wasn't a positive.

"Don't worry. I don't know anything." Joe grinned. "But I like to stay informed."

Ryan wasn't sure what kind of response, if any, was right.

"Can I give you some advice?"

"Sure. Of course." Ryan was always open to advice.

"If I have one regret, it's that I didn't choose different priorities. All of this?" Joe gestured back to the house. "It's nice, but it'll never make up for the years I lost with Cynthia. If I could do it again, I'd chase after her and choose her above success. Above the money. Love? That's so much more important than anything you win at the end of a contest. So make sure she knows how you feel. All of your feelings, even the scary ones."

Ryan nodded. She knew, didn't she? Maybe he needed to track her down and tell her again more clearly.

Jess scooped Meowth up and nuzzled her face into his fur. Who would have thought a long weekend in Florida at a billionaire's home could be an awful experience. Not her, that's for sure. And yet . . .

Maybe awful was overstating things some, but still.

"What am I supposed to do, Meowth?"

He looked at her, made a grumpy noise, and wriggled free of her arms.

"Well, that's no help." Jess sighed. There was a lot to do. She should run the wash. The cat litter would need scooping after three days away. Water the plants. "First up, fresh water for you. And a treat, because you're a good boy."

She left her suitcase by the front door and went into the kitchen. There was still plenty of water in his dish, and the steady but tiny stream of water trickled from the sink, too. He'd probably only used the fountain. He preferred it. She couldn't blame him.

Jess grabbed his dishes and dumped them out. She gave them a quick wash and refilled them before setting them back down on the little mat that marked off Meowth's eating area. He pounced on them like a starving man.

She chuckled. Silly cat.

She spent the next hour puttering around her condo doing chores and actively not thinking. About anything. Especially not about Ryan.

She cringed.

What was she supposed to do?

The knock at the door startled her. Jess glanced at her

pajama pants and oversized T-shirt before she checked the peep. Eyebrows lifting, she unlocked the door and pulled it open. "Christopher."

"Hey, Jess." He peeked around her, craning his neck. "You alone?"

"Given that the only person likely to be here is your roommate, I imagine you can answer that."

Christopher shrugged. "Just checking. I figure I shouldn't assume things about you anymore now that you're all grown up. Besides, Ryan isn't home."

He wasn't? She bit back the twenty questions that leapt into her mind. Christopher probably didn't know the answers. And if he did, he'd just smirk at her. She stepped out of the way and headed toward the kitchen. "You want tea?"

"I don't know why you ask me that. No. I don't. I don't like tea. I don't think I ever will." He followed her.

"Did you shut the door?"

"Duh." He rolled his eyes and sat on one of the stools she kept tucked under the short end of her kitchen island.

Jess kept her hands busy filling her electric kettle and plugging it in. She hunted through her tea stash, and finally settled on a soothing herbal that she scooped into a pot. She set a strainer over the top of a mug. It was just enough time for the water to boil, so she unplugged the kettle and filled the pot. Now it had to steep. Which made it hard to keep procrastinating. She turned to face her brother. "So. What brings you to my humble abode?"

He sighed. "Look. I'm sorry. Okay?"

She wanted to ask for what. Their parents had always insisted on much fuller apologies than that. At the same time? She wasn't sure she wanted all the details—what if he wasn't sorry about the right things? She shrugged and turned back to the teapot.

"C'mon, Jess. Don't be like that."

"Don't be like what, exactly? I don't know what you're sorry for, okay? Are you sorry you jumped straight to pregnancy? Or you're sorry that you got mad that I was dating a guy who you yourself have told me for years is the best man you know? Or is there something else in there that you're looking for me to forgive?" She poured tea over the strainer into her cup, tapped the strainer twice before setting it aside, and turned to face him, cradling the hot ceramic in her hands.

"That's fair. Can I say all of it, or do you need the whole formula?" He cocked his head to the side. "I know my words hurt you. In the future, I will try to pause and reflect before I speak."

She managed a small smile before taking a sip of the hot tea. At least he remembered some of Mom's apology formula.

"Are things okay between you and Ry?" Chris's face was the picture of concern.

Her belly tightened. Jess set the tea aside and she shook her head. "I don't think so, no."

"Because of me?"

"Sort of? Or maybe because your reaction made him say things that made me stop to think and, I mean, he's talking about forever. We've been dating what, maybe six weeks? He's already thinking about marriage? Who does that?" What was that clawing at her throat? Why couldn't she breathe normally? It happened every time she let herself think about Ryan's words.

She wasn't ready.

She might never be ready.

Marriage was a big deal.

"I'm confused. You've known him practically your whole life. It's not like you're strangers. So, of course, he's thinking that. I was thinking that—it's half the reason I flew off the handle. I'm not ready to think of you being married when you're my annoying kid sister who still tags along behind me, desperate to keep up and show that she's just as fun as a brother would've been."

Jess snorted. "It's been a long time since I was that kid."

Christopher shrugged. "Not in my brain. Then suddenly I have to deal with the reality of the beautiful woman my sister has become, and it was a lot to take in."

"I guess I can see that." Hadn't Ryan said similar things when the relationship between them changed?

"But Jess? Ry's a good man. I don't think I could choose a better match for you. Why are you suddenly freaked out?"

"If I could answer that, don't you think I wouldn't be freaked out anymore?" She picked up her tea and took a gulp, scalding her tongue. Dang it.

"You need to talk to him. The two of you are friends, first and foremost, right?"

She sighed. "Probably. Yeah."

"So?"

"So, friends talk things through." She ran a hand through her hair. "What if—"

"What if the sky falls? Don't do that. Just tell him how you feel. What you're thinking. This is Ryan we're talking about. He's going to understand. He's the best guy I know."

Hot tears filled her eyes. It was true. "Tied for first, for me."

"Aww." Christopher stood and crossed to her. He pulled her into a hug and patted her back. "You helped me when I was having trouble with Stephanie. I'm grateful for that. I love you. And I love Ry in a manly, platonic way."

Jess snorted out a laugh. "You're such a guy."

"I hope so." Christopher kissed the top of her head and stepped back, grinning. "Tell him how you feel. Go from there."

"I guess I can give it a shot." She frowned and reached for

her tea. If Ryan hadn't gone home, where would he be? "Oh, duh."

"Duh?"

"I think I know where Ryan is."

Christopher nodded. "Then I'll let you get to it. You might maybe mention that I came by and fixed things with you? That way, he knows it's safe to come home."

"You're still going to have to apologize to him. You know that, right?"

"Yeah, yeah. But I'm not doing Mom's thing. That's just annoying." Her brother grinned. "Love you, sis."

"I know it. Same goes." Jess waited until she heard the front door click closed behind her brother before she dumped her tea in the sink. Should she change? It felt like a lot of effort when they were just going to talk. It wasn't like Ryan hadn't seen her in her kicking around the house clothes before, either. Ugh. She was annoying herself.

Jess grabbed her phone and keys, slipped on shoes, and headed down to the basement gym. In Florida, he'd taken to going on long rambles down the beach. They didn't have the sand and waves here, but he could ramble as long as he wanted on one of the treadmills.

If he wasn't there . . . she'd have to corner him at work tomorrow and talk to him then.

The gym wasn't a happening place on Sunday night. But Ryan was ambling along on the treadmill. He'd been at it a while, if the sweat on his shirt was any indication. He hadn't turned on music or any of the TVs, so the only sound was the slap of his sneakers on the belt.

Jess moved into his line of sight and lifted her fingers. "Hey."

Ryan nodded once and pushed the Stop button on the treadmill. "Hi."

"I'm sorry."

"Okay."

She didn't bother to sigh. "Can we talk?"

"Isn't that what we're doing?"

Jess reached up and rubbed the back of her neck. He probably wasn't *trying* to make this hard, but he was definitely managing, anyway. "Are you angry at me?"

"Angry isn't the word I'd choose. Confused would work. Frustrated. Those sorts of terms." Ryan grabbed a towel and wiped his face. "What's going on, Jess?"

"I don't know. I'm confused, too. You pushed and pushed about telling Christopher—and then he blew up like we both knew he would, and you seemed surprised. Like really, what did you think he was going to do?" She should probably add something about the fact that he'd come and apologized this evening, but she couldn't quite get the words out.

"Honestly? I was less concerned about what he was going to do than what you were thinking." Ryan reached for her hand. "I love you. I've tried not to for so long that it took me a minute to realize that you were on board. But once I did? I wanted to shout it from the rooftops. And you wanted to hide everything behind closed doors. Why is that?"

Jess hunched her shoulders. How was she supposed to know? She could spin a story about wanting to keep it special— hold their relationship private and snuggly to herself. But that wasn't the truth. Or not the bigger part of the truth, anyway. So what was? "I was scared."

"Of me?"

"No. Never."

"Then what?" Ryan tossed the towel toward the gym's hamper and looked around the empty room. "Did you want to go into the TV room and see if it's empty? It'd at least be more comfortable."

No. No, she didn't. "Sure. I guess."

He gestured for her to go first.

Jess felt like she was dragging her feet as she plodded across the black spongy tiles that made up the gym floor. She tugged open the door and turned down the hallway that led to the common area full of TVs, couches, and a pool table. Maybe someone would be having a party and they'd have to cut their conversation short. Or kids could be using it—there were teens sometimes who would gather informally down here.

It was quiet. That wasn't a good sign. And, in fact, the space was empty. Jess headed for an oversized chair and flopped into it, tossing her legs over the arm so she was sideways.

Ryan lifted his eyebrows and settled on the last seat of a nearby couch. "So. You were scared, but not of me. So what were you scared of and, I guess, are you still?"

She nodded.

"I see."

"How can you? I don't even understand it. It doesn't make sense. You're the only guy I've ever had strong feelings for. Everything should be easy now—you're a dream come true. I have you. I have this amazing job. It's all perfect."

He didn't speak for a moment.

Jess's cheeks heated.

"Maybe that's the problem."

She frowned. "What do you mean?"

"Understand that I've spent a lot of time thinking about you. Watching you—not in a creepy way." He flashed a grin. "More like in an honorary big brother who's trying not to think of you as anything other than a sibling kind of way."

Jess chuckled. *That* she understood, at least. "I spent a lot of time doing that myself."

"So we know each other really well, would you agree?"

She nodded.

"And so when I say I love you and want to spend the rest of

my life with you by my side, you know I mean it. I'm all in. My decision's made, and I have no plan to change it." He held her gaze as he spoke.

And there it was, that clutch in her chest that made it hard to breathe. Even as the rest of her wanted to melt, there was that other part of her urging her to flee. She swallowed, but it did nothing to ease the dryness in her mouth.

"That's what scares you. I think, maybe, you were in love with the *idea* of me. Because I was safe and out of reach. And now that it's real, you don't know what to do." Ryan's gaze darted away.

Jess frowned. Were there tears in his eyes?

He pushed to his feet and put his hands in his pockets, but his arms bounced. If he hadn't been wearing jogging pants, she would have thought he had change in his pockets that he was jangling. "So here's the thing. I can't go back. I can't just rewind and pretend none of this happened. I love you, Jess. I love knowing that. I love the freedom of letting those feelings out into the open. So I'll wait."

"You'll wait?" It was like she was scrambling to catch up while he raced ahead of her into impenetrable darkness. "What are you saying?"

"I'm saying you need to figure out what you want. I hope it's me. I really do. But until you're sure, I think we need to limit our time together to what we need for the contest at work. I think that's about all my heart will be able to take. I love you, Jess. When you figure out what you want, you know where to find me." He turned and strode in long, even strides from the room.

Jess's breath hitched. Her hand flew to her mouth and tears spilled from her eyes, but the lump in her throat was too large for sound to work its way around.

She closed her eyes and gave in to the sense of falling into a dark, bottomless abyss.

10

I t had taken a solid week for Jess to get past the feelings of shame and awkwardness at work when she had to deal with Ryan. They were working on the March deliverable for Joe and Tyler—an assessment of their strengths and weaknesses. All she saw in herself were the latter.

Ryan was friendly and polite, but he'd retreated behind the wall of "Christopher's friend" that kept him separate.

It was like she'd lost a part of herself.

Once or twice, she'd caught him looking, and thought—for the briefest moment—that she glimpsed sadness and longing. But as soon as he noticed her, Ryan was back to clowning around. It was an effective means of keeping her at arm's length. No one got close to a clown—the clown wouldn't let them.

Now, Jess avoided Ryan unless they had an appointment for the contest at work. It was just easier.

And a lot less painful.

And if it didn't alleviate the confusion that clouded her brain, it at least allowed her to push it aside to deal with at some point down the road in the nebulous future. That was good enough for her.

It had to be.

For now, there was plenty of work to do, and getting lost in the details of a server was preferable to thinking.

A throat cleared behind her. "Excuse me. Are you Jessica Ward?"

Jess swiveled in her desk chair and cocked her head to the side. "Sure am. Jess. How can I help?"

"I'm Holly. Holly Bell. I'm with SociaLinks?"

Jess nodded. She didn't have a ton of dealings with the social media app people, but she recognized Holly from the meetings with Tyler every month. "Sure. You're part of the contest."

"Yeah. But this isn't about that. I was talking to Aaron and he kind of blew me off, but he said if I was really concerned to talk to someone in Cyber. So here I am."

"Here you are. Do you want to sit?" Jess pointed to her guest chair. What was it going to take for Holly to get to the point?

"Oh. Sure. Thanks." Holly came into Jess's cube and sat. "Um. I don't know if you know how we're set up. Or maybe it doesn't matter. But we use cloud servers for all the hosting. So the app connects up that way."

"Right. That's pretty common these days. Standard, even. Very few people want to bother with in-house server farms when the big warehouses are more affordable and have experts on-site. Are you having trouble with the server farm? That's not really what we do, but I can try to take a look. That said, there's probably tech support if there's a physical issue that needs to be investigated."

"No. At least I don't think so." Holly clenched and unclenched her hands. "Sorry, I'm really bungling this. I think our servers are under attack."

"Oh? Now that *is* something we do." Jess grinned. Maybe the work she did today wasn't going to be as boring as she'd been anticipating. "Tell me what makes you think that."

Holly breathed out a relieved-sounding sigh. "Okay. Part of what I do every morning is a quick traffic check. It's good data for all our stats—and those stats feed feature rollout and marketing and just everything."

"Sure. Stats make the world go round."

"Seems like it, doesn't it?" Holly offered a shy smile. "Anyway, Aaron thinks I'm overreacting, but there's been a big spike two days running. Two a.m. And it's not recent. The big one, yeah, two days, but there have been smaller ones that were still outside the realm of normal, I thought at least, for maybe a month? I dug into the IP addresses a little and they just seem hinky."

"Hinky." Jess bit her lip. It definitely sounded like something worth investigating further.

Holly's cheeks reddened. "Sorry. I have a weird vocabulary. Everyone says so."

"Don't worry about it. It's a cool word. I'm happy to look into it."

"Oh. Thank you. I went ahead and created you an account with admin access because I was hoping I could convince you to take a look." Holly handed Jess a sheet of paper with the details she'd need. "Could you change the password when you get in, though? I don't like knowing a default is out there, even when it's something I made up."

"Absolutely." She would have even if Holly hadn't asked. The idea of writing all this down was like bugs under her skin. It was better than emailing it, but there were ways to set up accounts and notify new users—and require password changes on login. Of course, from what Jess remembered from her little foray into the backgrounds of everyone who was part of the contest, Holly was a programmer, not a system administrator, so maybe she didn't know that. "It might take me a little time. I can come find you when I know something."

"Oh. Right. Ha." Holly stood, her hands flitting at her sides. "I appreciate this. I can figure out a charge code if you need me to. I don't know how stuff like this—you helping me when we're not in the same division—is going to work when the contest ends. Will we be more separate companies?"

Did she want an answer? She wasn't leaving, so maybe. "I'm not sure. But since Joe's not really spinning us all off on our own, more just setting a stronger management structure so he doesn't have to stay so hands-on with everything, I imagine this will still be able to happen. There'll still be interdivisional overhead. I use those codes periodically. I'll just find the one for Social and use it, if that's all right?"

"It should be. I'll double-check and let you know if it isn't."

"That works." Jess smiled. "It might be tomorrow. I may need to see the spike in progress to trace and track more accurately."

"Do what you need to do. And if you come back and need to tell me it's nothing and I'm paranoid, that's okay."

Jess chuckled. "Good to know."

"Okay. Well, bye." Holly waved and slipped out of sight.

Jess shook her head and spread the sheet of notebook paper on her desk, smoothing out the creases from where Holly had folded it. Might as well give it a look now and see if it was something that was going to be an easy fix. Half the time, someone had left a cron job scheduled or something like that. Easily explained—or removed—when it was identified. But then there were actual attacks.

And social media? Those were ripe for targeting. All that delicious personal information to harvest. People left their credit cards attached to accounts, birthdates, and sometimes even social security information. It was a dream for hackers looking to do some identity theft. Heck, even if that data was encrypted and well secured, just being able to create a large quantity of fake accounts that impersonated real users and then use those to do social engineering was a big bonus. The fact that the Nigerian prince email scam still worked was a testament to that.

Jess flexed her fingers then got to work.

Who had set these servers up?

After a few minutes poking around, Jess opened a desk drawer and dug for a clean notepad. She clicked her pen a couple of times before starting a list. The people at Social needed to hire Cyber to audit their systems. Hmm. That actually was something they ought to offer to all of the Robinson companies.

Jess flipped to a new page in the notepad and quickly scribbled her thoughts on what that type of service ought to include. It would probably need to be a new branch within Cyber, if only because they were fairly stretched in terms of personnel already. Contracts were definitely the bread and butter of their business —but offering this in-house, quarterly audits maybe? Plus monitoring and rapid response?

She'd take it to Ryan and they could . . . oh, right.

Jess blew out a breath. She'd type it up as an email and send it to Ryan. Should she copy Joe on it? Probably. Joe liked to be in on this sort of conversation from the start rather than being brought up to speed later. Or at least, that was the vibe she got from him.

Maybe he was trying to change that with this contest to find new upper-level management for each branch. But with something like this, something that was going to require cross-branch participation? He'd want to know. At least she would, if she were Joe. Either way, she'd include him on the email. If he said go with it but leave him out of future convos, then she'd do that.

Jess drummed her fingers on her keyboard. She really wanted to talk to Ryan about it to flesh out the ideas beforehand.

Why hadn't she thought through—like all the way—the ramifications of starting something with him before she'd done it? It was just like her. Take the hacking activities. She'd really only considered one of the possible outcomes. The good one. She sure hadn't considered that the FBI would still be trying to pin nefarious intentions on her.

Now, both situations had turned out horribly.

What did she do?

This was work related. Ryan had said they should still have work conversations. And they had been, albeit stilted ones.

Maybe step one was to finish this thing for Holly. Then she could worry about everything else.

Maybe by then, her prayers about Ryan would have stopped bouncing off the ceiling and she'd know what she was supposed to do about the personal aspects of their relationship.

Please, God. I need help.

~

"RY? DO YOU HAVE A MINUTE?"

Ryan looked up and studied Jess. She looked completely normal. Was this bothering her at all? He'd had three different people each day asking him if he was sick. Apparently, he was washed out and had circles under his eyes. Who knew not sleeping would do that. Oh, wait. "Did we have an appointment?"

"No. I can come back. Just tell me when." Jess started to turn.

"It's fine. Come in. I was making sure I hadn't missed something." Smooth. Way to make her feel unwelcome. Things were awkward enough without him finding new ways to screw it up. "What's up?"

Jess clutched a notebook to her chest as she took halting

steps toward his guest chair. "So, yesterday, Holly Bell came by to see me."

He frowned. "Holly . . . she's in Social?"

"Yeah. You've always had a good head for names and faces."

Probably because he'd spent so much time studying her and all the people in her life, trying to decide if there would ever be room for him. "Thanks."

"Sure. So anyway, Holly noticed some traffic spikes that she couldn't explain and asked me to take a look. It got me thinking. So I put together some thoughts." Jess offered the spiral notebook to him.

Ryan didn't reach for it, so Jess set it on the edge of his desk.

"Thoughts about what? A traffic spike? I guess I'm not following why this brings you to my office." He bit off his words. What was wrong with him? He'd said they were still going to have work conversations. This was one. But it felt contrived. Like she was looking for a reason to sit with him, and he couldn't take it. The scent of her soap had already infiltrated his senses, and he wanted nothing more than to drag her onto his lap and kiss her like a drowning man searching for air.

But that wasn't going to fix anything. At this point, it would make things worse. Ryan was prepared—or trying to be—for Jess to realize that she didn't want him after all. Kissing her before she decided was asking for it to hurt even worse than it already did.

"Oh. No. I guess I skipped that. Internal audits, basically. We're all Robinson companies, right? So why isn't Cyber monitoring Social's servers? We could easily stand up a team who did monitoring and rapid response for the various Robinson arms. If they already have the sysadmin doing it, we could either talk about bringing them over or it would be something to take off their plate and free them up for work that's more in line with what they probably anticipated doing when they were hired."

She nudged the notebook closer to him. "I outlined the idea in here."

"It's a good idea." Why had no one thought of it before now? "A very good idea."

"Yeah?"

He smiled at the hope in her voice, but quickly straightened his features. Work friends. Not even life friends. Ryan was friends with Christopher right now. Period. Especially since Chris had finally made an actual apology—one that included the realization that Ryan was the perfect man for his sister. Not that it helped at this point, but it made Ryan feel a little less crazy. He reached for the notebook and flipped it open. He skimmed the outline, nodding as he made his way down the page. "You really thought about this."

"Once I got started, yeah, I couldn't seem to stop." Jess shrugged.

He nodded. He was having that problem right now, too. Anything to keep his mind off her. Off the relationship he yearned for. Was that what occupied her thoughts? Or was she going over how close she'd come to ending up with him and counting it a lucky break? His gaze darted up and locked with hers.

Hurt shone out of her eyes.

Ryan looked away. He couldn't be the one to fix this, no matter how much he wanted to be. Jess needed to choose him, all the way. He couldn't settle for less. "You should write it up and email it to Joe. I'd be very surprised if he didn't put you in charge of heading it up. It's a good plan."

"Oh. As it is? I was hoping you might have some ideas to add —or that you'd see somewhere I missed something?"

"Jess. This is good. Is there room to improve it? Probably. But Joe doesn't need everything perfect—in fact, I imagine he'll have ideas of his own once you present it to him. I did see one thing—"

"Yeah?" She leaned forward, eager.

Ryan flipped the notebook around and pointed to the section where she talked about payment between the divisions to cover the employee time. "I think—maybe—we ought to allow for hour-to-hour trades."

Jess drew her eyebrows together. "Trade?"

"Sure. Like, if Social wanted to fix up our web pages to make them more in line with a cohesive corporate theme, then we could trade them the hours they spend on that for the same number of hours of one of our techs. Or do it by billable cost rather than hour, to account for salary differences."

"Everyone needs Social to do that for them."

"They do." Ryan frowned. "In fact, we should suggest that as a footnote. There has to be something that could be traded to Social for that sort of internal web work no matter what division. Well, maybe not the game developers."

Jess grinned. "Actually, they could put together an in-app exclusive game for the platform. That'd be a huge marketing bonus and would set them apart from the other social media apps out there. Maybe it wouldn't attract everyone, but it wouldn't push current users away. If the game studio targeted a younger demographic than is currently on the platform? I bet Social would eat it up."

"Smart. Put that in there. If we can come up with suggested trades for each branch, it might help sell the idea."

"Why do we care?" Jess pulled the notebook close and jotted in the margin.

"It feels like it'd be an accounting nightmare to move money around internally like that. The tracking isn't really different, but trades would cut down on actual overhead expenses all around.

Probably." Ryan shrugged. Maybe Joe wouldn't go for that sort of setup, but it seemed worth suggesting. "Joe might still say no."

Jess nodded. "He could say no to the whole idea. If he does, I still think Social needs to hire someone to handle the security. These traffic spikes are definitely purposeful. I haven't figured out where they're coming from yet, but I'm going to."

"Okay. Make sure you track the time and put it on the right overhead account on your timecard."

"Will do. I checked with Holly, and she says I have the correct number for that."

"Great." Ryan thought of and discarded twenty additional things to say.

The silence was apparently long and awkward enough that Jess stood. "Thanks. I'll copy you on the email, if that's okay? I feel like you should be in the loop."

"I'd like that." Ryan cleared his throat and stood. He tucked his hands in his pockets to keep them from reaching for her. "I think I'm finished with the review we needed to do for Tyler. I'll send it to you for feedback?"

"Yeah, okay. I wish—"

"Please, don't." A lump formed in his throat and he shook his head. "I love you. That isn't going to change. But I'm not going to push you to feel something you don't."

"Ryan." Her shoulders fell. "It's not that—I do—it's just—"

"Exactly. Keep me posted on the network spikes, too, would you? If someone is targeting them, it's possible that we're going to start seeing attacks in the other branches. We need to be proactive about looking for them. I'll send you that report for Tyler. If you make a lot of changes, would you shoot it back to me first, before sending it in?"

"Of course. Bye." Jess pressed her lips together and held his gaze for two long heartbeats before she shuffled from his office.

Ryan closed his eyes and sank back into his desk chair.

Why did everything have to be so hard?

This was the right thing. The mature thing. He had peace when he prayed about it—when he prayed about Jess. Ryan had to believe that God was going to bring her back to him, but it was still so hard. Because what if the peace was just God's way of saying that He was going to be with Ryan, even if Jess, ultimately, was not?

11

Ryan scrolled on his phone. The TV was streaming some sort of blacksmithing competition, but it couldn't hold his interest. Neither did any of the various social media sites he had a marginal presence on. Christopher was off with Stephanie doing something—probably just dinner and kissing. That was what he always seemed to walk in on when they were over here. They insisted they were getting lots of work done for the competition as well, but, whatever.

It was good his friend was happy and in love.

Knowing Christopher, he was already shopping for the perfect engagement ring.

Ugh.

Ryan switched over to his calendar. There was nothing major on it at work tomorrow. Maybe he'd call out. It wasn't a complete fabrication to say he didn't feel well. The problem, of course, was that "heartsick" wasn't something that sick days were supposed to be for. Mental health day? That was honest. It wasn't as if he used his sick leave often.

Or maybe he should visit his family. They were in Colorado

these days. Now that Dad had retired, he and Mom had settled in what used to be the summer vacation cabin. They'd made it through a winter, so it must be okay, but getting snowed in all the time was definitely not Ryan's idea of a good time.

They should be past that now, though, shouldn't they?

Easter was coming up. Just about two weeks out. Hmm.

He searched for flights to Colorado and considered the options. They were doable. It might be fun to surprise everyone and get away at the same time. He could stay for a week and reset. He probably shouldn't miss the first Monday of April meeting with Tyler for the contest, which would mean he'd be flying home on Easter Sunday. He adjusted the dates and frowned. There were afternoon options that would work. He'd be exhausted on Monday, but that was nothing new at this point.

"I'm doing it." Ryan dragged himself off the couch and padded to his bedroom. He grabbed his laptop out of its bag and set it up on his desk, then repeated the flight search. He added a rental car to the package and clicked "Buy."

It didn't take long to get the confirmation email.

He updated the office vacation calendar and sent a quick note to Tyler and Joe with his plans. Maybe he should have gotten permission first, but it was too late now. There shouldn't be a problem. The only potential issue would have been with the Monday meeting. But he'd be back for that.

His email dinged.

It was just Tyler reminding him to have the self-evaluation turned in before he left. He tapped out a quick reply that it was nearly complete. It shouldn't be an issue to get it turned in by the end of this week.

Jess had sent it back with a few notes. Maybe he'd look at it now and just get it done. Then he'd be free and clear and not spend the next week stressing about whether or not he'd make that deadline before he had to leave.

The door buzzer sounded.

Ryan frowned and headed back down the hall. There was no reason for anyone to be visiting. They knew some of their neighbors in a wave-when-they-passed kind of way, but no one came over looking for a cup of sugar. Chris and Jess both had keys. The guys from Bible study would call first.

He looked through the peephole. Seriously? Ryan jerked open the door. "Special Agent Mosby. To what do I owe the pleasure?"

"Mr. Foster, can we come in?"

"No. State your business." Ryan leaned against the doorjamb and crossed his arms. This was his home. They weren't going to sully it with their presence. Not when they were doing their best to smear Jess's reputation. It didn't matter that he and Jess weren't together. He was still—always—going to protect her when he could.

"Are you sure that's a wise position to take with me?" Mosby stepped closer.

"If you're hoping to intimidate me, you don't. What do you need?"

"Mosby." The second man was back. He laid his hand on Mosby's arm. "Mr. Foster, it really is rather sensitive. I imagine you'd be more comfortable in your condo."

"No. I wouldn't. Seeing as how Mosby is fond of trying to sneak listening devices into places, you'll understand that I'm not willing to have him anywhere near my home."

The man's lips flattened, and his gaze darted to Mosby. "Are you aware that Ms. Ward is online for more than two hours every night between one and three a.m.?"

"Yes." Jess had been keeping him up-to-date—by email, rather than coming in person, but that was probably better anyway—on her attempts to isolate and identify the traffic spikes for Social. She'd also noticed that there were staggered spikes on the game dev servers and the business apps. He didn't have to be a suspicious person to see a pattern with that sort of data. Joe had actually reduced her daytime hours to give her the freedom to work while the attacks were underway.

Mosby's eyebrows lifted. "And do you know what she's doing?"

"Yes." Ryan wasn't giving them more information than they needed.

"Care to share?" Mosby's mocking tone was grating.

"I'm sure you can figure it out, since you're watching her so closely."

"Mr. Foster." The other man spoke up, his voice steady and calm. "You can understand that we're just doing our jobs, yes? Keeping an eye on potentially dangerous activity is what we're charged with."

"Nothing she's doing has any potential for danger. In fact, her activity is at the behest of Joe Robinson and directly related to an internal security audit."

"You can't seriously expect us to buy that." Mosby jerked away from his partner's grasp. "We know she's ShadowWarrior. We know she's planning an attack."

Ryan shook his head and made eye contact with Mosby's nameless friend. "I'm not sure Mr. Mosby is well. I'll be contacting Amanda McDow as soon as we're finished here. I imagine she'll be in touch with your superiors shortly thereafter. You need to stop this witch hunt and start chasing actual crime."

Mosby sputtered.

The other man shook his head. "I'm sorry you're not willing to be reasonable, Mr. Foster."

"I could say the same thing." Ryan stepped back into his condo and began closing the door. "Have a good evening."

He shut the door on their protests and double-checked the locks before reaching for his phone. He'd call Ms. McDow. Then

Joe. Then Jess. His stomach clenched. Maybe he should go up and tell her in person? No.

In fact, maybe it was better to have the lawyer get in touch with Jess. The two of them probably needed to talk, anyway. So he'd call Amanda and Joe and then he'd do something else to keep his mind off how badly he wanted to talk to Jess.

To hold her.

Gah. He had to stop. She was fine. She was a grown woman.

And she had a decision to make.

No matter how much he missed her, he wasn't going to push. Because he was all in. And he wanted her to be all in, too.

JESS PACED HER LIVING ROOM, phone to her ear. Her lawyer was ranting in Jess's ear about the visit Mosby and his silent pal had paid to Ryan. Sounded like he'd shut them down, which was lovely, but in this case, she wasn't even doing anything remotely wrong.

"Amanda. I'm doing my job. This is for real what I get paid to do. The owner of the company knows what I'm doing and why and supports it one hundred percent, because we need to get to the bottom of why our systems are under attack." Jess paced to the kitchen and paused long enough to see that Meowth's food bowl was empty. She walked to the tin where she stored the food and scooped some out. "I have something I'm going to try tonight that should let me untangle it. I honestly believe tomorrow morning I'm going to have this hacker by the ears."

"Am I the only one who doesn't see a coincidence between you getting another FBI visit and the fact that your servers are getting attacked, or am I paranoid?" Amanda blew out a breath. "The judge is dragging his feet on my paperwork, because no one wants to go up against the FBI. But I'm serious, Jess, we have to keep fighting this. If I can't push this through, I'm thinking we need to sue Mosby personally."

"Can we do that? He's a federal employee doing his job. Isn't that protected?" It seemed like it should be, otherwise everyone would sue the IRS when they got audited.

"Depends on whether or not what he's doing is actually required as part of his work. I've got some feelers out. We're going to get this guy off your back. I promise."

"Don't promise things, Amanda. You can't guarantee that." Jess sighed. It would be nice if her lawyer *could* promise things. Jess would grab hold and never let go. But if her trial had taught her anything, it was that justice could be slippery when public opinion got involved. "Look. You keep doing lawyer things. I'll keep doing my job. And maybe Mosby will get it through his head that he's barking up the wrong tree."

"I have to ask. I don't want to, mind you, but I feel like I need to know. Have you been doing any more extracurricular activities?"

"No." She'd thought about it. Especially since Ryan had ended things with her. Or put the ball in her court. Or whatever he'd done. She had too much free time now, and digging around for a new target sounded like a great way to fill her evenings, but she knew better. It wouldn't do anyone any good to have ShadowWarrior out there drawing Mosby's attention. Although, maybe going silent was fueling his fire, too. Who knew how to read someone like him?

"Good. Keep it that way." Amanda sighed. "I like you, Jess, but I don't make a habit of taking on guilty people."

"You're a defense attorney, isn't that kind of your job?"

Amanda laughed. "No. I'm choosy. It's not just about winning. It's about being righteous when I do it. I'm not sure I could live with myself if I got someone truly heinous out of their well-earned punishment."

"I know. It's why I hired you. Clients do research, too, you know."

"As long as we understand each other. I'll touch base again tomorrow or the next day. Stay out of trouble, and if Mosby shows his face near you, you call me. Night or day."

"I will. Thanks." Jess ended the call and set her phone on the island. It was early yet to get on and start watching the servers. If she was on now, she'd be tempted to dig around some more and see what she could find on Mosby. That had been her intention from the beginning, but Ryan had asked her not to and . . . well, he was probably right about that. Still. It sure would be nice to fight fire with a little flame of her own.

Unless it blew backwards, and she ended up being the one getting burned.

So that was off the table.

Her email dinged.

Ryan. Her heart sped up. Was he done being stupid? Finished punishing her? She wanted him to come back and tell her that they were all right. If he'd pull her into his arms, everything would be fine and they could pick up where they left off. Things were okay between her and Chris. From the little Christopher said—and it was *very* little—things were okay between him and Ryan as well. So why couldn't things be fine between Ryan and her?

He wanted her to choose him. Hadn't she done that? Okay, fine, she'd had a moment after Christopher's blowup. That was to be expected, wasn't it?

She tapped to open the email and frowned.

LOOKED OVER THE SELF-EVALS. I THINK WE DID A GOOD JOB— WE'RE DEFINITELY NOT SUGAR-COATING ANYTHING. I MADE NO CHANGES TO YOUR LATEST VERSION, SO IF YOU'RE OKAY WITH IT, I'LL SHOOT IT TO JOE AND TYLER. LET ME KNOW? ~R

That was it?

Her heart sank. She tapped out an affirmative and set her phone down. Why did it hurt even worse when he was distant and polite? Was this what their relationship was going to be going forward? Colleagues? Not even super friendly ones?

Jess sighed and headed over to the computer she used when she worked at home. It was more suited to her covert operations. Tonight, she was going to figure out the traffic spikes. She had no idea how to solve the problem with Ryan. Or with Mosby. So this was the one thing she might be able to influence, and she was going to give it her all.

She pulled up her monitoring software and let it run on one screen while she opened a game in another. A little hacking and slashing with a sword might be a decent way to pass the time except . . . what was that? She enlarged the monitoring window. There was a little bump of traffic. Was that happening every night? She pulled up the historical data and looked. Sure enough, there were little bumps four or five hours each time there was a larger push later on. How had she missed that?

She hadn't been looking.

And it wasn't unreasonable for traffic to go up now. Dinner was over, people were settling in for their evening entertainment. Social media would for sure be part of that. But . . . coincidence was never a good thing.

Jess got Tor running and created a new disposable identity to use while she dug around. Maybe it was nothing. Maybe she'd see it was all Mr. and Mrs. Suburbia getting online to share cheesecake recipes and gripe about baseball.

But maybe it wasn't.

Five hours and two energy drinks later, Jess pushed away from her computer and pressed her fingers to her burning eyes. She couldn't stop the triumphant grin. He was sneaky, but she was sneakier.

Now, the question was how to handle it.

She wanted to package it all up and send it anonymously to the woman at the FBI that she'd been leaking information to. But . . . every time she did that, Mosby got on her case. Which meant either that woman was sharing the info, or Mosby was spying on her. Hm. That might be easy enough to find—especially now that she knew how to evade his ham-handed traps.

She took another half hour to poke around. Finally, she found what she was looking for and documented the steps. She might share it. She might not.

She needed to call Amanda.

But she wasn't going to do that at—Jess paused to check the time and laughed—almost four a.m.

She stood and stretched her arms up over her head. Meowth opened one eye and gazed balefully at her.

"I know. I'm sorry. Let's get some sleep." Jess ruffled his ears before turning to shut down her computer. Maybe rest—and a conversation with her attorney—would give her the next steps.

She wanted to talk to Ry.

Jess crawled into bed and dragged the covers up over her body. Why was he being so stubborn?

She blew out a breath, flopped over onto her back, and stared at the ceiling. Why was she?

He hadn't walked away. Not really. She'd pushed him. Because it was easier than admitting she was scared. She'd been scared to change things between them. Scared at the prospect of Christopher finding out. Scared when Ryan started talking about forever.

Now she was terrified of a forever that *didn't* have Ryan in it.

Tomorrow—well, later today—she was going to have to fix a lot of things.

12

———

Jess glanced at Amanda. "You're sure?"

"I'm sure. Calm down." Amanda studied Jess before smiling. "How long has it been since you wore that skirt and blazer?"

"I don't know. It's for funerals and job interviews. So it's been a while. Why?" Her professional clothing options were limited. They weren't something she enjoyed wearing, so she owned exactly two choices. Both basic and black.

"Your shoulders are a little dusty."

"Oh. I thought I shook all of that out." Jess brushed at her shoulders and frowned. "I can go—"

"Special Agent Orbison will see you now." The admin looked up from her computer with a bland smile.

"Thank you." Amanda stood, leather portfolio in her hands, and nodded to Jess. "You're fine. Come on."

Nerves danced in Jess's belly as she followed Amanda into the office. Amanda had assured Jess that this was the right person to talk to, but Jess didn't know anything about him. What if . . . well, there were a lot of "what ifs" that played through her brain.

"Amanda. It's good to see you." Orbison's smile was warm and genuine. He was older, grey at the temples, and he looked like he should be someone's grandfather. Oh, he was fit, but still gave off that cuddly warm vibe Jess associated with loving grandparents. He turned his gaze on Jess, steady and assessing. "You're Jessica Ward."

"Yes, sir." Her palms were slick with sweat, but wiping them on her skirt was probably the wrong move. She curled her fingers.

"It's nice to finally meet you. I've heard a lot."

Jess snorted.

Orbison smiled. "Not all of it from Special Agent Mosby. So some has been quite complimentary. In fact, did you know you have a standing job offer here?"

Her eyebrows lifted, and she shook her head.

"I didn't imagine you did. But it's common knowledge, around here at least, that if your résumé gets posted we're supposed to do what it takes to get you on board. I don't imagine you're looking currently?"

"No, sir."

"Well, it was a long shot." He cleared his throat and gestured to the chairs in front of his desk. "Have a seat and tell me what brings you to my office."

Amanda waited until Jess was sitting before taking her own seat. "I've kept you apprised of Mosby's harassment of my client."

Orbison's lips thinned, but he nodded.

"Last night, he visited Ryan Foster, one of Ms. Ward's coworkers, and made some of the usual threats. Mr. Foster contacted me. I got in touch with Jess. And Jess, in the course of doing her job overnight to unravel some recent traffic spikes on some of the Robinson Enterprises servers, traced back the activity to these accounts." Amanda opened her portfolio and withdrew a sheet of paper from the top of the stack. She offered it to Agent Orbison.

He took it and gave it a casual glance. Then his gaze zoomed back to it and frown lines furrowed in his forehead. "I see."

Amanda's grin was sharp and toothy. "I thought you probably would. Jess has additional documentation to back that up, if you'd like to follow her discovery path. It seems Special Agent Mosby has been a rather busy boy in his off hours. Doesn't he know attempting DDoS attacks is illegal?"

Orbison looked up and studied Jess. She fought the urge to fidget. "Are you sure you don't want to come work for us?"

"I quite like my job. But thank you." Jess twisted her fingers together in her lap. He believed her? Just like that? She looked over at Amanda.

Amanda gave Jess's arm a reassuring pat. "I'll leave the documentation with you. Jess also has had some information come into her hands that suggesting Mosby is spying on a handful of your cyber-crime agents."

Orbison's eyebrows shot up. "That's a serious accusation as well. There's proof?"

Amanda offered more paper across the desk.

Orbison glowered at it as he flipped through. "I see. Well. You've made my day a little bit worse, but I can safely tell you that Mosby will not be bothering you any longer, nor will anyone else continue his delusional manhunt. I'll see to it that the matter is closed. That's not a free pass, mind you, so keep your nose clean."

Jess nodded, fighting the urge to hunch her shoulders. Something in there must have given him a nudge that some of Mosby's suspicion was correct. "Yes, sir."

"And keep in mind that we have a unit full of agents whose job is to dig through the underground and sniff out the bad guys. You could be part of that legally. Just say the word."

Her cheeks heated. Yeah, he definitely suspected. It wasn't even tempting, though. Everyone knew who the feds were. The cyber-crimes people always gave themselves away. "I appreciate the offer, but no, thank you. That said . . . maybe I could arrange a seminar to show them ways to be more effective. They're a little clumsy."

He laughed. "You mean they stick out, despite trying to blend in."

"Yes, sir."

"I'm going to take you up on that. But let's let things die down some here first. I'll be in touch."

"Do you need my—never mind. Of course, you don't need my contact information." Jess's cheeks burned.

Amanda chuckled. "He can always call me, if he can't get it on his own. Thanks, Uncle Fred."

Uncle Fred? Jess shook her head. No wonder Amanda had managed to get on his calendar so quickly. She stood and shook his hand when he offered it.

"It was nice to meet you in person, Ms. Ward. I hope, some-day, to have you on my payroll. Don't say no again. I don't think I could take it." He winked.

Jess smiled. She didn't want to work for the FBI. Ever. But it was nice to know that maybe, just maybe, they'd be off her case now. "It was good to meet you. I'm serious about helping your people blend in."

"I know you are. I'll be in touch." He leaned across the desk to kiss Amanda's cheek. "Tell my brother he still owes me ten dollars."

"Dad says he didn't lose that bet. You're going to have to take it up with him." Amanda grinned. "See you."

Orbison's chuckle followed them out of his office.

Jess turned to Amanda as they headed back to her car. "Thanks."

"Hey, it's what you pay me for."

True. And it was likely Amanda's bill was going to eat a big chunk out of her savings. It'd be worth it. "Does he try to get you on staff, too?"

"Only constantly. He doesn't understand that I like helping the underdog." Amanda shrugged. "I tried to tell him there was no way you'd say yes, but he was adamant he had to try."

"I don't mind. It's kind of flattering. But I like where I am. What I do."

"Who you work with?" Amanda sent her a sly grin. "Ryan Foster hits high on the hot scale."

"He does."

"It might not be my business, but I'm going to say it anyway. If you're not doing everything you can to hold onto him forever, you're an idiot. And if that's the case, then you're also my first major miscalculation when it comes to choosing clients. Don't ruin my streak by being stupid, okay?"

"I'll see what I can do. Out of curiosity, why do you think I'm not?"

"Because he called me and told me to call you last night. And I could tell it killed him. Because he wanted to call you and tell you to call me instead."

Jess nodded. She'd wondered about that. "I hurt him, I think."

"So fix it." Amanda shrugged. "He's a guy. It should be pretty easy."

"You'd think that, wouldn't you?"

Amanda laughed. "You've got it bad. Love always clouds our vision. Look, pray about it—then act. Because the two of you need to be together. Anyone with eyes can see it."

Jess frowned. She had eyes. And okay, fine, she could see it. She hadn't wanted to, but that didn't mean it wasn't there.

RYAN EXITED the jetway and forced himself to exhale. He'd spent the last week studiously avoiding Jess, and it was torture. He missed her. Everything about her.

Christopher said he understood, but Ryan could tell he didn't. His best friend was too deeply in love. Even though Christopher and Stephanie had had their own struggles getting to this point. Still, Ryan had seen engagement rings on Christopher's monitor more than once, so things were definitely working out for his friend right now.

Lucky jerk.

Ryan chuckled at himself. He didn't begrudge Chris happiness. He just wanted some of his own. With Jess. But until she decided it was what she wanted, too? He wasn't going to cave. This was too important. He didn't want to coast. Or be strung along until he was forced to realize that they wanted different things.

Please, God, don't let her truly want different things! I feel so strongly that she's who You want me to marry, I don't know what I'll do if it turns out I'm wrong.

He made his way through the airport, got his rental, and settled in for the drive to his parents' cabin. Mile-wise, they weren't far from the airport, but the mountain made it a bit of a trek. Still, Colorado was always beautiful, so it wasn't a hardship.

Finally, he reached the turnoff for the cabin and switched from pavement to gravel. His rental bounced along. He winced. Was he going to get dinged for paint scratches? Maybe he should have ponied up for the insurance after all.

The trees parted as he eased around the bend in the driveway, and there was the cabin. The log A-frame jutted up into the trees and sunlight glinted off the windows. Smoke wisped out of the chimney.

Ryan grinned.

He parked beside his parents' beat-up SUV and climbed out.

The door opened, and his mom's face morphed from curiosity into elation. "Honey! Come quick, Ry's here!"

He couldn't have stopped the laugh if he'd tried as his mother bounced down the steps and threw herself into his arms. "Oh, baby. Why didn't you tell us you were coming?"

"I wanted it to be a surprise." He squeezed her tight. "Surprise."

She laughed and leaned up to kiss his cheek. "Best surprise ever. How long are you here?"

"Let go of your mother and give me a hug." Dad's voice boomed out from beside his mom.

Ryan released his mother and hugged his dad. As a teenager, he'd always rolled his eyes when Dad would drag him into full contact, squeezing hugs instead of the detached side hug that he'd wanted. Now? He soaked it in. This was love. Unconditional. Accepting. Welcoming. He wanted to give the same to Jess—that and more. "Hi, Dad."

"Your mother asked you a question. I think it's time to answer." Dad stepped back and his gaze roamed over Ryan's face. "You're not in trouble, are you?"

His lips twitched. "Not the kind you're asking about."

"Oh." Mom clapped a hand to her heart. "You have girl trouble. Finally. Tell me all about her, and I'll tell you how to fix it. Maybe Ryan's going to give us grandkids after all, honey."

"It's Jess."

That was all it took. Mom and Dad exchanged a look before Mom's eyes filled. She turned and hurried back to the cabin.

"About time." Dad patted Ryan's shoulder. "We'd about given up on that. We would love any woman you chose. You know that, but we've always prayed it'd be Jess. Come on in and tell us what happened. Then, I'm sure, your mom will know what you need to do."

Ryan clicked the trunk release and reached for his duffel. He slammed the lid closed and turned to look at his dad. "I left the ball in her court. I'm not sure if she even wants to pick it up."

Dad nodded thoughtfully. "That's a pickle. Come in and tell us the story, anyway. If nothing else, it might help to get it off your chest."

Ryan snorted. It wasn't as if he'd been keeping it bottled up. He went on about it to Chris every time his friend asked. But maybe Mom and Dad would have insight he was missing from other quarters.

He stepped into the cozy cabin and dropped his duffel beside the stairs. It was warm, and the air was permeated with the rich aroma of coffee and cinnamon. His mouth watered. "Are there still cinnamon rolls?"

"You always did have a nose for baking. Yes. Your mom still cooks like you live at home. I try to hold up my end, but I can't just eat six cinnamon rolls in one sitting anymore." Dad patted his newly trim belly. "Not now that I got that belly back under control."

"If it makes you feel better, I probably can't, either. But one would sure hit the spot." Ryan slid onto a stool at the overhanging counter that served as a pass-through into the kitchen from the living and dining room combination.

Mom slid a plate across to him and followed it with a mug of coffee done just the way he liked it. "You never mentioned that anything had changed between you and Jess. When?"

He thought through the last several months as he took a big bite of cinnamon roll. He chewed and washed it down with a sip of coffee. "Late January, I guess. I told you we were a team for the contest at work."

Mom nodded.

Dad slid onto the stool beside Ryan and accepted the mug of coffee Mom handed him.

"Although maybe things were already starting to shift before that. I know my feelings were—at least subconsciously. But I was doing okay keeping them to myself. My fear of Chris's reaction helped."

Dad chuckled. "How'd he take it?"

"That's kind of part of it all. She didn't want him to know. I went along with it at first, because, yeah. Bad news, right? But then it started to be like sneaking around, and when he asked me what was going on and I lied, I knew we had to come clean."

Mom reached across to cover Ryan's hand. "Of course you did. I'm surprised you were able to handle hiding it at all. Subterfuge has never been one of your innate skills."

Ryan snickered. It was true. Mom and Dad had always caught him when he'd tried to pull a fast one. It was like they knew before he did—which apparently translated to his feelings about Jess. "Anyway, he lost his mind. Jess freaked out. I told her she needed to choose what she wanted. And now I'm waiting."

"What do you want?" Dad swiveled, his gaze meeting Ryan's as their knees bumped under the counter.

"Everything. Forever. Marriage, kids, the whole ball of wax. That might have freaked her out even more." Ryan took another bite of cinnamon roll, but it tasted like dust as he chewed. His heart ached. "Stepping away—or back—was the hardest thing I've ever done."

"You proposed?" Mom's hand covered her mouth.

"No. But I told her I wanted forever. She knew what I meant."

Dad nodded. "She's a smart girl. Always has been. Hang on, I'll be right back."

Ryan watched Dad slide off the stool and plod over to the stairs. He grabbed Ryan's bag and carried it up with him.

"Where's he going?"

Mom shrugged. "You know your father."

"Uh-huh. So do you. But it's fine. I'll wait."

Mom smiled. "You really love her, don't you."

"I do." Ryan drank more coffee. "I didn't think it was supposed to hurt."

"There's always a little pain with love, because it means someone else has the power to ruin you. But they can complete you in ways you didn't know you were lacking, too, so in the end, it's always worthwhile." Mom squeezed his hand before moving to the fridge and opening the door. "I wasn't planning for company, so we're pretty plain, food-wise, around here."

"Plain's fine. What do you think I eat at home?"

"A lot of takeout, I imagine."

He laughed. "You're not wrong."

"Here we are." Dad came down the last step and back to the counter. He smacked a box on the granite and slid it over to Ryan before getting back onto his stool. "Been saving that for you for too many years now."

Ryan's eyebrows drew together. He opened the lid to reveal a smaller, royal blue box that appeared to be velvet. "Is this . . .?"

"Take a looksee. If you don't want to use it, it won't hurt our feelings."

"Yes, it will." Mom came back over to join them. "I'll get over it, but my feelings will definitely be hurt."

Dad laughed.

Ryan grinned and upended the box into his hand. He flipped it open and nodded. "I remember these."

"I should hope so. I wore those a lot of years." Mom stroked the top of the wedding set. "Then your father upgraded me for our thirty-fifth anniversary. Don't be like him and wait. Twenty-five would've been better."

"Yes, well, you have expensive taste, and I couldn't afford it at twenty-five, could I?" Dad chuckled.

Mom grinned at him.

Ryan's throat clogged. He could picture the ring on Jess' slender finger. It would look fine with her no-nonsense short nails. Even when she painted them strange colors on a whim. Gosh, he wanted that. He wanted to be with her, on the couch, while she pulled out all the smelly nail polish bottles and set to work. He closed his eyes.

What if she didn't choose him?

Ryan closed the ring box and put the lid back on the cardboard box that held it. "Thanks, Dad. I hope I get to use it."

Dad bumped Ryan's shoulder. "We'll pray that you do. Now, hurry up and eat that cinnamon roll. I've been trying to teach your mom to play checkers, but she's hopeless. I could use a game that's actually competitive."

Ryan laughed, and the tension in his body eased. "You're on. It's good to be home."

13

"This is an April Fool's Day joke, right? Come on, Ry, where are you really?"

Ryan shook his head and cradled the phone to his ear with his shoulder as he stood on the back porch of his parents' cabin. "Colorado. With my folks. I'll be back for the Monday meeting."

"I'm not worried about that. Well, okay, I was a little. I need you there. 'Team' implies more than just me." Jess's voice was grumpy—like a toddler woken too soon from her nap. "But I need to catch you up on some stuff."

"I still have email and everything here. Modern marvel."

"Don't be a jerk. I don't want to send you an email."

He choked back several versions of "I don't want" responses and tried to keep his voice calm and level. He breathed in the crisp, Colorado air. "Then you'll have to wait until Monday after the meeting."

Jess growled. "Are you trying to punish me?"

"No." He could answer that honestly. He wasn't going to be upset if she saw it that way, sure, but he hadn't set out to do it. Still, anything that got her closer to an actual decision was good.

"Fine. Be that way. I'll see you Monday, I guess."

"Jess." He closed his eyes, hating the hurt that he heard. "Are you okay?"

"Yeah, I'm okay." She sighed. "I miss you."

"Good." He winced. "I didn't mean—I'm not trying to push. This isn't easy for me, either. You have to know that."

"I guess."

"I love you."

Jess was quiet long enough that Ryan pulled his phone away from his ear to see if it was still connected.

"I know."

He snorted out a laugh. "Really, Han Solo?"

"Yeah, well. Had to be done at some point, didn't it? Nerd."

"Takes one to know one."

Her laughter ended on a sigh. "I really miss you. Monday? For sure?"

"Monday for sure. Bye, Jess." He ended the call and set his phone on the porch rail. Maybe he should give in. They could still have a relationship, couldn't they? They could be with each other while she figured it out.

Except then he'd never know if she was sure or if she just went along with it because it was easier than letting go.

No. It was too important. He wasn't going to pressure her into anything. No matter how badly he wanted to.

"It's nice out here." Dad came to stand beside him and look out over the mountainside. "Your mother and I like to sit out in the evening and watch the stars."

"That would be pretty. It's probably dark enough to see quite a few."

Dad nodded. "Helps you realize just how small we are, in an eternal sense. And makes it all the more clear that God's love for us is amazing. Why, when the universe He created is so vast, does He care about me?"

"And my inconsequential problems with love?" Ryan slung his arm over his dad's shoulder. "Thanks, Dad."

"What I'm here for. You okay?"

"Maybe? She misses me. That has to count for something."

Dad chuckled. "It's a good thing. Be kind of awful if you came all the way out here and she didn't even notice. You didn't come here as a test, did you?"

"No. Chris knew where I was going and when. It's on the shared calendar in the office. I didn't hide it. I just didn't specifically tell her."

"It's out of character for you to take a vacation spontaneously."

"I can be spontaneous."

Dad shot him a bland look. "Oh yes. Your mother and I are constantly concerned with how you hare off willy-nilly all the time."

Ryan frowned. "Careful, old man."

"Ooh. Now I'm scared." Dad shook his head. "Come on, your mother's baking cookies. Let's play checkers until they're out of the oven."

"I can do that. You're sure you want to lose again? Seems like it might be demoralizing at this point."

"Boy, you might want to watch yourself. There's no law that says I have to let you sleep in my cabin."

Ryan laughed. "Sure there is—its name is Mom."

"Hm. That's a point."

Lighter in spirit, though still aching for Jess to hurry up and see that being with him was what God wanted, Ryan sat on the couch and spun the checkerboard around. "We'll mix it up. You can go first. Maybe it'll be an advantage that'll help keep you competitive."

"Watch it, buster." Dad studied the board and made his opening move.

Ryan still won, but it was close. It was always a good game. Dad had the ability to think several moves out, something he'd taught Ryan when he was young. Ryan leaned away from the board and tented his fingers. "And so the student has become the master."

Dad laughed.

Mom carried a tray of cookies to the coffee table, chuckling as she did. "He's going to be glad to see the back side of you."

"Mom's not wrong. When do you leave again?"

"Sunday after church." Ryan reached for a cookie. "I wanted to come for Easter, but with the first Monday of the month meeting, I couldn't stay."

Mom rubbed his shoulder and perched on the cushion beside him. "I'm glad you came. It's been too long since you did."

"I'm sorry." He needed to do better. He could get busy and forget the priorities that mattered. This contest hadn't helped any with that—which was probably the opposite of what Joe wanted them to be learning. "I'll try to do better."

"Well now, it's not as if the planes don't fly both directions." Dad shot Mom a look. "There's nothing to say we can't come visit you. Like for a wedding. Or an engagement party. Baby shower."

Ryan laughed and held up his hands. "Okay, okay. We'll see what Jess has to say about any or all of that."

"Will you live in Jess's condo when you're married? It's just one bedroom, right?"

Ryan shook his head at his mom. "What part of that is 'waiting'? I haven't even thought that far. But probably? I mean Chris could afford the mortgage without me, and he's the one who bought the condo. I'm just a roommate renter. And, your need for grandbabies aside, I don't think we'd actually be hurrying to start a family."

Mom patted his knee. "Don't wait too long."

"All of this hinges on Jess's deciding that loving me is what she wants to do."

"Well, she's a smart girl—always has been. She'll figure it out." Dad took a cookie and bit into it.

Ryan studied the cookie in his hand. Jess was definitely smart when it came to computers. He wasn't so sure about how well she was willing to trust her heart.

JESS PULLED over to the side of the road and scowled at the GPS on her phone. This couldn't be right. She'd been driving up the side of the mountain for what felt like an hour. And fine, the clocks on her phone and the dashboard of her rental car said it was just twenty minutes, but time should go faster in places where there were hairpin curves.

Six miles to her destination.

If she could make the drive without having to pull over to throw up. Who knew it was possible to get carsick while driving?

This was insane.

Ryan would be home on Monday.

She could have waited.

But when she'd talked to him on Thursday, and he'd said he loved her, she'd just known. She loved him. Of course she did— she'd even said it to him. But she *loved* loved him. She wanted it all—the ring, the wedding, the babies. Her cheeks heated. Practicing to make the babies wouldn't be so bad, either.

Getting through the day at work yesterday had been torture. She'd almost caved and changed her flight three times. Maybe she should have, but she was here now, and the red-eye flight had made the most sense when she'd booked it.

They'd have all day today and most of tomorrow before they had to fly home.

Christopher had relented and given her the flight information for Ry's return flight, so they'd be on the same plane home. He hadn't had the seat number.

Maybe that was a good thing? If this went horribly wrong, it would be even worse knowing she had to sit beside him with no escape on a metal tube hurtling through the sky.

Jess eased back onto the road and followed the phone's instructions. The final turn, where the pavement changed to gravel, left her sighing with relief.

She'd made it.

Please, God. Don't let him turn me away.

She parked beside what was clearly a rental car—nearly a twin to the miniature sedan she drove—and stepped out, her heart in her throat.

Her shoes crunched on the rocks as she crossed the cleared area in front of the cabin to the steps up to the porch. The A-frame building suited the Fosters. She'd seen pictures of the place from Ry's vacations. Had her family joined them once or twice? Maybe. It felt like they might have, but her memory was fuzzy.

She reached up and knocked briskly on the door.

Then she waited.

Jess turned to glance over her shoulder. There was another, older SUV parked out there as well. It was possible that the Fosters had two cars though, and they'd all gone off on an adventure.

Or they'd seen it was her and were pretending not to be home.

She knocked again, louder.

Jess slipped her phone out of her pocket and stared at it. She could call him. And say what? Come answer the door, moron?

Faint footsteps echoed inside.

Jess knocked a third time.

The footsteps came closer. Finally, the door opened.

Her heart fell at his feet. Did he see it? Could he know?

"Hi." Lame lame lame. Nice opening, Jess.

One corner of his mouth poked up, and he leaned against the doorjamb. "Just happened to be in the area?"

A bubble of near hysterical laughter worked its way out. "Something like that."

"You want to come in?" His eyebrows lifted.

"Maybe. I just had something I needed to tell you."

"And it couldn't wait until the Monday meeting?"

Jess shook her head. "No."

"Sounds serious."

"Definitely."

"You'd better come in, then." Ryan stepped back and gestured for Jess to go ahead.

Jess stepped through the doorway, and slipped past Ryan. He closed the door. She turned. "Yes."

"Yes what?"

"To everything. To anything. I want it all. With you. I love you, even though it's terrifying. Maybe because it's terrifying. Because it's always been you, and it's always going to be you."

Ryan's lips curved. "Hold that thought."

Jess blinked as he walked off. Hold that thought? Really? She turned to watch as he crossed the open living and dining area. He grabbed something off a counter and started back.

She crossed her arms. "Are you doing this to punish me?"

"Never." He took the lid off a cardboard box and looked up. He held her gaze. "Say it again."

Her heart thundered in her chest, but her voice came out as a whisper. "I love you, Ryan Foster."

"I love you, too." He shook a small velvet box out of the slightly larger box, flipped it open, and took out a sparkling ring.

Ryan reached for her left hand and started to slide the ring onto her finger. "Let's get this where it belongs."

Jess swallowed. She knew this ring. "This is your mom's ring. I can't take her ring."

"Dad got her a new one for their thirty-fifth. She really wants you to have this one." Ryan's gaze was steady on hers. "So do I."

"Me, too!" Ryan's dad's voice called from somewhere else in the house.

Jess and Ryan both started to laugh.

"So much for that moment." Ryan shook his head.

Jess reached up and cradled his face in her hands. "No. It was perfect. I love you, Ryan Foster. And even though you've never actually asked me to marry you, I want you to know I will. I want to be yours forever, and I want you to be mine."

Ryan lowered his head so his lips hovered over hers. "We'll be each other's."

EPILOGUE

Four months ago, at the company Christmas party.

Holly Bell smiled as the company owner, Joe Robinson, put an engagement ring on his cardiologist, Cynthia's, finger. It was like something out of a fairy tale. The perfect ending to a perfect evening. A harmless fantasy about a long-lost love coming back into her life wasn't going to hurt her. Even if she knew fairy tales were only in books and movies and never happened in real life.

Well, they didn't happen in *her* real life.

She listened as Joe continued talking about choosing new day-to-day heads for each branch of his company so he could step back and have more time to spend with his new bride. Her heart melted. This fairy tale kept getting better and better. Wouldn't it be a kick if she were chosen to be on one of the teams?

It was unlikely. Stuff like that—the *good* random stuff—didn't happen to her. And she didn't really see where being chosen to compete for a promotion could end up as a bad thing, which meant her name wasn't likely to be in the running.

She glanced around the room. If she were in charge, who would she choose to compete for Social? Her gaze landed on Aaron Powell. Oh, yeah. Aaron was on that list, no question. He was everything a social media customer experience manager should be. All schmooze and gloss and shiny, white teeth. But he got the job done. She had to give him that.

Holly didn't know him. She didn't really know a lot of people in her office. She came in, did her work, and went home. She would have skipped this party if the memo hadn't made it sound like optional attendance wasn't actually optional. She needed a job. The fact that she liked this one made her want to hold on to it.

So she'd hired a sitter, even though Luca, nine years old going on nineteen, had insisted he didn't need one. And here she was. It was worth it to see that ring and the joy on both Joe's and his fiancée's faces.

Holly settled back in her seat, content to watch as the DJ started up music for dancing. That wasn't her scene. Not anymore. Once upon a time, she'd had some good moves. But unlike her sorority sisters, whose moves had landed them boyfriends who eventually turned into husbands, Holly had gotten Luca out of it. And nothing else.

Well, they were fine. Maybe she missed out on a lot of his milestones because she was working to provide for them, but she wasn't going to turn into a desperate single mom on the prowl for a husband. She could take care of herself and her boy.

He was her everything.

It sure would be nice to get that promotion.

Maybe . . . maybe she'd see what she had to do to be considered, after all. She might not be Joe's first choice, but she could prove herself if they gave her the chance. Her gaze swung back to Aaron Powell and her resolve strengthened. Could she beat him? Holly wasn't sure.

But boy, she'd love the chance to try.

FIND out what happens next in So You Have My Secret Baby

ACKNOWLEDGMENTS

I'm so grateful for readers who continue to take a chance on my books. I'll admit, when I got the idea for this sort-of-billionaire series, I had a lot of doubts. I saw (and continue to see) tons of comments in online reader groups that basically talk about how they would never read a billionaire book. So thank you for being willing to take a chance!

I'm also so grateful to my family - my wonderful hubby and boys - who put up with the mercurial moods of the writer-mom who makes tacos for the fourth night running because that's the kind of mental energy she has left. (Although, let's be clear, tacos are always a good idea. Am I right?)

I'm also grateful to my writer friends - Valerie Comer and my author squad girls in particular. Thanks for being you.

Most of all, none of this would work without Jesus. And that applies to so much more than writing.

WANT A FREE BOOK?

If you enjoyed this book and would like to read another of my books for free, you can get a free e-book simply by signing up for my newsletter on my website.

OTHER BOOKS BY ELIZABETH MADDREY

So You Want to Be a Billionaire

So You Want a Second Chance

So You Love to Hate Your Boss

So You Love Your Best Friend's Sister

So You Have My Secret Baby

So You Need a Fake Relationship

So You Forgot You Love Me

Hope Ranch Series

So You Love Your Best Friend's Sister

Hope for Tomorrow

Hope for Love

Hope for Freedom

Hope for Family

Hope at Last

Peacock Hill Romance Series

A Heart Restored

A Heart Reclaimed

A Heart Realigned

A Heart Redirected

A Heart Rearranged

A Heart Reconsidered

Arcadia Valley Romance – Baxter Family Bakery Series

Loaves & Wishes

Muffins & Moonbeams

Cookies & Candlelight

Donuts & Daydreams

The 'Operation Romance' Series

Operation Mistletoe

Operation Valentine

Operation Fireworks

Operation Back-to-School

Prefer to read a box set? Find the whole series here.

The 'Taste of Romance' Series

A Splash of Substance

A Pinch of Promise

A Dash of Daring

A Handful of Hope

A Tidbit of Trust

Prefer to read a box set? Get the series in two parts! Box 1 and Box 2.

The 'Grant Us Grace' Series

Wisdom to Know

Courage to Change

Serenity to Accept

Joint Venture

Pathway to Peace

Prefer to read a box set? Grab the whole series here.

The 'Remnants' Series:

Faith Departed

Hope Deferred

Love Defined

Stand alone novellas

Kinsale Kisses: An Irish Romance

Luna Rosa (part of A Tuscan Legacy)

Non-Fiction

A Walk in the Valley: Christian encouragement for your journey through infertility

For the most recent listing of all my books, please visit my website.

ABOUT THE AUTHOR

Elizabeth Maddrey is a semi-reformed computer geek and homeschooling mother of two who lives in the suburbs of Washington D.C. When she isn't writing, Elizabeth is a voracious consumer of books. She loves to write about Christians who struggle through their lives, dealing with sin and receiving God's grace on their way to their own romantic happily ever after.

facebook.com/ElizabethMaddrey

instagram.com/ElizabethMaddrey

amazon.com/Elizabeth-Maddrey/e/B00A11QGME

bookbub.com/authors/elizabeth-maddrey

Made in United States
Orlando, FL
05 May 2022

17555235R00104